Dalton's Vengeance

When rancher Cliff Sinclair offers the homesteaders of Two Forks three dollars for an acre of their land, Dalton thinks the deal is just too good to be true. But most of the townsfolk are delighted to take this apparently generous offer – Dalton and his friend Loren Steele are the only ones to say no.

Sadly, Dalton discovers he was right to be suspicious when Cliff's hired gunslinger, Frank Kelley, kills Loren and runs Dalton out of town. So begins Dalton's quest for vengeance that will test his survival instincts and the speed of his gun-hand to the very limit.

By the same author

Dalton
Dalton for Hire
Deputy Dalton
Dalton's Bluff
Dalton's Valley
Dalton's Mission

Dalton's Vengeance

Ed Law

A Black Horse Western

ROBERT HALE · LONDON

© Ed Law 2011
First published in Great Britain 2011

ISBN 978-0-7090-9169-1

Robert Hale Limited
Clerkenwell House
Clerkenwell Green
London EC1R 0HT

www.halebooks.com

Typeset by
Derek Doyle & Associates, Shaw Heath
Printed and bound in Great Britain by
CPI Antony Rowe, Chippenham and Eastbourne

CHAPTER 1

'Can you smell something burning?' Dalton asked.

Loren Steele laughed then pointed at the fire roaring away in the fireplace.

'I should hope so,' he said.

'I didn't mean that.' Dalton sniffed again, but this time he could no longer detect the acrid whiff that had concerned him. He dismissed the question with a wave and returned to the matter in hand. 'Perhaps Cliff Sinclair's deal has got me feeling edgy.'

'And me too. It's just too good to be true.' Loren leaned forward to poke the fire, as if the comforting flicker would give him an answer that had alluded them during their two-hour discussion. Flames flared and he warmed his hands. 'I keep coming back to the fact that our land isn't worth three dollars an acre.'

'It isn't, and as no man in his right mind would make such an offer, there has to be a catch. Perhaps Cliff knows something we don't about what'll happen when the railroad reaches White Falls.'

Loren shrugged. 'If that is the case, then good luck to him. He'll deserve the money he'll make from his gamble while we'll all walk away with five hundred dollars, and that'll be a great start in setting up somewhere else. . . .'

Loren trailed off and sniffed.

A moment later the same odour that had worried Dalton earlier drifted by, this time stronger than before. Dalton looked around searching for its source while Loren glared at the fire then shook his head, dismissing it as the culprit.

With a quick gesture Loren indicated that he'd go outside while Dalton checked the backroom.

Dalton did as requested, but before he'd reached the backroom door, Loren threw open the front door and located the source of the trouble.

A fire was burning on the porch. It was only a pile of branches and twigs, but the strong wind was whipping the thin stream of flames up above the height of the door.

While Loren looked for a broom to push the fire away, Dalton ran into the backroom and gathered up a blanket. When he reached the porch, the open door had helped to fan the fire and the flames were licking at the doorframe with an insistence that would take hold of the timber house within moments.

'Who'd do something like this?' Dalton said as he

joined Loren.

'We're the only two men who oppose Cliff,' Loren said.

He gave Dalton a long stare. Then both men concentrated on dealing with the fire. Loren slipped outside for as far as he was able while avoiding the lick of flame. Then he shoved the larger burning logs off the porch while Dalton slapped the patches of burning wood on the building.

With a few flicks he smothered the nearest flames then joined Loren in slipping outside. To his relief there were only a few patches where the fire had caught hold of the wooden walls and it had yet to reach the cedar shingles.

Even better Loren had already pushed the largest logs away. Now he was using the broom to sweep away the last of the embers.

'If this was Cliff's work,' Dalton said as he slapped the wall, 'he didn't do it very well.'

'This was a warning. The next time he won't give me a second chance.'

Loren batted the last of the embers off the porch then kicked dirt over them. When that smothered the flames and plunged them into darkness he swung round to look into the darkness, a hand to his brow.

His home was two days' steady riding west of the town of White Falls and was amongst a dozen homesteads that bordered Cliff Sinclair's land. They'd called the area Two Forks when they'd first arrived. But with White Falls attracting the most settlers and with the railroad set to pass through that town, it was becoming increasingly unlikely that the settlement would grow, even before Cliff's offer to buy them all out.

The nearest homestead was Dalton's a hundred yards away. Dalton joined him in looking for any sign of movement there then from the main settlement.

'Can't see nothing,' Dalton said after a while, 'but that doesn't mean nobody's out there.'

Loren nodded then turned to the door.

'Agreed. I'll get my rifle. You finish off here.'

Dalton tore himself away from looking for whoever had lit the fire and turned back to the wall where the short break had let the patches of fire grow. He stood beside the largest and slapped it hard with the blanket while Loren went inside.

Loren had managed a single pace through the door when he uttered a cry of surprise. A gunshot tore out. Two staggered footfalls sounded. Then Loren wheeled out through the doorway clutching his belly.

He removed the hand and looked at the blood dripping through his fingers. A curious expression appeared, as if he were examining a hand that wasn't his own. He looked at Dalton and met his gaze, his mouth opening to say something, but the words didn't emerge.

Loren keeled over to land on the porch he'd built himself and where for the last three years the two men had often spent a quiet but sociable evening. He jerked once then stilled.

Dalton stared at his form, unable to accept that after all they'd been through together his good friend had been killed. They had both reckoned that Cliff Sinclair would give them plenty of trouble if they continued to stand in his way, but neither man had expected it would end like this.

Shuffling sounded within the house, breaking Dalton out of his shocked fugue. The footfalls closed on the door then stopped, giving him the impression that whoever was inside had picked a position that let him check on Loren while staying hidden.

Slowly a six-shooter emerged held in an outstretched hand. Clearly the man inside was unsure where Dalton was. Dalton was unarmed and so he stayed beside the wall, watching the doorway through the flickering flames that continued to spread.

The man stopped moving at a point where his arm protruded up to the elbow. Then he turned to go back inside, but he turned away from Dalton, and so seizing that as his best opportunity to take him on, Dalton launched himself forward. In two long paces he reached the doorway then swung in to find he was facing the man's back.

He just had enough time to note that the killer wasn't Cliff Sinclair. Then, with two bunched hands

9

held together, he directed a swinging blow at the back of the man's neck.

At the last moment the man detected the planned blow and jerked away. Dalton's swipe still caught him a glancing blow to the shoulder, knocking him aside, but the force he'd exerted also made Dalton bend double and stumble for a pace.

He stuck out a leg to right himself then turned to take on Loren's killer, but his assailant had got his wits about him quickly and he bundled into Dalton then shoved him back against the wall. Heat rippled against his back as the developing fire burnt through the wall.

In desperation he pushed himself away. A table was before him and in his haste to get away from the hot wall he slipped on a wet patch of what was probably blood and fell.

He made to grab for the table, but he only succeeded in upending it. Plates and the empty iron pot that had contained their earlier meal went crashing down with him.

Dalton sprawled on the floor in an ungainly heap. Quickly he shook off the debris then spun round to his knees aiming to kick off from the floor and leap at his assailant. But when he turned it was to see that the man had picked up the pot by the handle.

The heavy iron utensil came swinging round in an arc. Dalton flinched away from it, but he must have failed to avoid it as the next he knew he was lying on his chest and a pain in his head was pounding with an insistent rhythm. The pot was sitting before him and all he could hear was crackling.

He moved to rise, but his arms refused to lift him and a nauseating burst of dizziness made him flop back down. So he lay gathering his breath with his cheek to the floor while he took stock of the situation.

The man who had hit him appeared to have gone. Dalton winced, accepting he must have been unconscious for a while and that made him look to the wall.

The sudden motion again made him dizzy, but what he saw forced him to get himself moving. The wall around the door was ablaze. Flames were spreading across the ceiling creating an undulating fiery blanket that was rapidly disappearing beneath the lowering smoke layer.

Unbidden Dalton coughed then forced himself into motion. He took a deep breath then crawled along beside the table, his head throbbing and his eyes stinging.

The smoke swirled blocking his view of the room and his back tingled from the heat. Working on memory alone he crawled to the backroom door and while still on the floor he pushed it open.

A welcome rush of cold air wafted over him from the open window, but that new source of air had the unfortunate effect of fanning the already lively fire in the main room. A blast of heat bathed his back making him yelp in pain.

As the smoke surged around him he forced himself to his feet, swayed, then set off with a determined tread for the window. This moved him away from the main fire, but that didn't slow him and he folded over the sill then fell to the ground outside.

While he gathered his breath he heard shouting. A surge of panic hit him as he wondered whether Loren's killer had accomplices. So he looked around for the best place to hide, but then forms emerged from the dark, their faces made haggard by the brightness of the fire.

To his relief they were the Two Forks homesteaders. The first to reach him was Chester Clarke, who owned the land beside Dalton's.

'Where is he?' he demanded. 'We can't see him.'

'You mean Loren?' Dalton murmured as Chester drew him to his feet and helped him away from the house.

'Who else? Pull yourself together while there's still time to get him out.'

'I'm sorry. It's too late. Loren is dead.' Dalton shook off Chester's helping hand to stand free. He faced the house, seeing that it was unlikely that the roaring flames could be beaten back. 'He was the first, but I'll make sure he's the last.'

CHAPTER 2

'So you didn't get a good look at this man, then?' Sheriff Blake said when Dalton had finished his tale about last night's events.

'I'd recognize him if I saw him again,' Dalton said, his tone sombre, 'but I'd find it hard to describe him.'

Last night, despite getting help from everyone who lived in Two Forks, he had been unable to defeat the fire. He hadn't made any progress in searching for the culprit either and with the house still smouldering this morning, he hadn't been able to recover Loren's remains before Blake had arrived after his pre-arranged trip from White Falls.

They were now standing outside Wes Potter's barn awaiting the start of the meeting.

'There's nobody new around that I know of.' Blake moved aside to let two people enter the barn. 'If he hasn't moved on, he'll stick out.'

'Forget about him for now and ask Cliff Sinclair what he was doing last night.'

Dalton hoped Blake's answer would be a different one to the responses the homesteaders had provided last night. Then, nobody had been prepared to accept that Cliff had anything to do with it, but the lawman should be more open-minded.

Blake considered Dalton. 'I know you've had a bad year, but don't accuse Cliff of murder. He's been in White Falls for the last few days. I played poker with him a few days ago.'

Dalton gritted his teeth, refusing to acknowledge that the tragic events of last winter had anything to do with him not liking Cliff.

'Does Cliff usually stay in White Falls to play poker with you?'

Blake acknowledged Dalton's point with a nod.

'No, but he was relaxed, so I don't reckon he was deliberately distancing himself from Loren's murder.' Blake shrugged. 'And either way, Loren had a colourful past. If even half the tales he tells of his exploits are true, many people will have a grudge against him.'

'His stories were tall tales to tell of an evening.' Dalton provided a rueful smile as he recalled some of the tales he'd told Loren of his own past, most of which were true. 'You'll need a better theory before I believe it wasn't Cliff.'

'I haven't got one, but keep your theories to yourself.' Blake waggled a finger at him. 'Cliff is a popular man and if you accuse him, it'll set people against you and drive them to support his offer even more.'

Dalton snorted. 'I didn't think Cliff had bought you too.'

'He hasn't. This deal doesn't affect me and so I'm keeping an open mind. All that concerns me is that you don't do something stupid that'll make it harder for me to prove who did kill Loren.'

Dalton accepted this point with a grunt and so in a more relaxed frame of mind he joined Blake in watching the last of the homesteaders arrive.

Although over the last few weeks Dalton had argued with many of them, last night's tragedy had ensured that nobody displayed the truculence that Loren and he had expected to face today. Everyone looked at him with sadness in their eyes and many murmured words of sorrow.

Despite this, Dalton still looked at everyone with scepticism as he searched for signs of anyone who was less distressed than the others were.

Nobody looked guilty and everybody met his eye, and so he filed into the barn with the rest. Dalton stood at the back with Blake while the families of the other dozen homesteaders took up positions nearer to the front where a long plank had been laid out over two barrels. Several short tree trunks had been rolled in and set upright to serve as seats.

For several minutes the people talked animatedly

to each other as they awaited the start. Presently the door at the back opened and two people came in. Silence descended instantly.

Mindful of Blake's warning, Dalton avoided looking at the entrants, but when they came into view he was surprised to see that although one of the men was Cliff Sinclair, the other was a man he hadn't seen before.

He glared at the newcomer, wondering if he were his attacker, but when the man sat at the front he saw that he was wizened and that he had the bearing of a meek official. He wore businesslike clothes along with small pebble glasses perched on the end of a nose that was sharper than the strip of land between the rivers that gave Two Forks its name.

Cliff sat and raised a hand to gather everyone's attention.

'I was sorry to hear of last night's events,' he said. He ran his gaze over the gathering and received supportive murmuring. 'Anyhow, I have been in White Falls finalizing the details with my attorney William Grout and hopefully today we can bring the situation to an amicable conclusion for us all.'

William had a valise thrust under an arm, which he placed on the makeshift table beside Cliff. Then, using a precise and earnest manner, he removed papers from the valise along with a pen, which he laid out.

Shuffling and mumbles of discontent sounded as

everyone waited to hear what he had to say, but this didn't hurry him as he moved each paper a few inches to the side until they were arranged to his satisfaction. Only then did he look up.

'Gentlemen,' he said in a reedy voice that forced everyone to strain their hearing to understand him, 'from now on you will deal with me and not with my client. Luckily, I am in a position to provide you with all the answers you will need.'

William looked around nervously with his shoulders hunched, as if this revelation might encourage someone to attack him, but then the barn door creaked and he breathed a sigh of relief.

Dalton glanced to the side to see what had pleased him. A new man had entered and he was standing just in from the doorway.

This man folded his arms and set his feet wide apart while glaring around in a show of him having been hired to look after the meek William. He didn't look at Dalton, but Dalton had seen him before.

He caught Blake's eye and gave a slight nod. Blake registered surprise with a raised eyebrow.

Dalton had expected that after completing his mission Loren's killer would be long gone. But now he was brazenly letting everyone know he worked for Cliff.

When everyone had considered the new man, with many squirming uncomfortably, William picked up a sheet of paper and read from it.

'As you know my client Cliff Sinclair wishes to buy the land within a mile of the rivers at Two Forks so that he has uninterrupted access to water. He is prepared to buy everyone out on an equitable basis. Cliff's offer was for three dollars an acre, but I am pleased to inform you that with the matter now becoming most urgent, that offer can be increased to four dollars.'

A cheer went up from some, gasps of bewilderment from others, but with an imperious raised hand William called for quiet. Everyone's interest was high, so he got that silence.

'This offer however,' William continued, 'has one provision.'

With William adding drama to the situation by putting down one sheet of paper and picking up another, several people shouted out.

'What provision?'

William continued at the same unhurried pace while peering at everyone over the tops of his glasses.

'Firstly, the deadline for agreeing to these new terms is sundown on the day after tomorrow. After that the offer will be withdrawn.' William coughed. 'Secondly, this offer must be taken up unanimously. If even one person dissents, then nobody will get anything.'

Silence reigned for several seconds as everyone waited to see if there would be more conditions, but when William opened up his valise and placed the papers inside, questions came thick and fast.

'Why within two days?'

'Why must we all agree?'

'What happens if we can't agree?'

William ignored the questions and packed away his papers. He tucked the valise under his arm and moved to go, but several people moved to the side to bar his way.

The new man considered the unruly gathering then walked to the front. He barged people aside to reach William, even though everyone was asking their questions in a good-natured way.

'You can't leave now,' Chester called out.

'Yeah,' Wes Potter said. 'You have to tell us why.'

'I will be leaving.' William glanced at the man who had now reached his side. 'I have provided the full details: sundown tomorrow, four dollars, must be unanimous. The only outstanding issue is for you to discuss this final offer amongst yourselves.'

With that pronouncement and with the body-guard at their backs William and Cliff left the barn. Within seconds it descended into pandemonium.

Dalton eyed the growing debate, noting that it didn't take long for everyone to turn to him, judging that he would be the main source of trouble over accepting this deal.

Blake moved forward to placate the townsfolk, but Dalton didn't feel inclined to face them now and so he followed the delegation from the barn.

Outside, he walked straight into the bodyguard.

'Now what are you doing?' the man demanded, holding his arms wide apart to ensure Dalton couldn't approach Cliff and William.

'I'm leaving,' Dalton said. 'Who are you to stop me?'

'I'm Frank Kelley.' He smiled, as if the name should mean something to him.

'Obliged to meet you . . . again.' Dalton waited for a response, but when it didn't come, he looked past Frank at William and Cliff who were now climbing up on to a buggy. 'I want a word with Cliff before he goes.'

Frank shook his head. 'His attorney said everything Cliff needs to say. I'm making sure he doesn't get troubled no more.'

'And will keeping trouble away involve you repeating what you did last night?'

Frank considered him calmly, but before he could respond Cliff spoke up from the buggy.

'Frank, come on,' he said. 'I don't have the time to waste.'

Frank stayed looking at Dalton for long moments before treating him to a sneer.

'I'll be watching you, Dalton,' he muttered. He headed to his horse and drew it up beside Cliff and William on the buggy. In short order the three men rode away towards Cliff's ranch.

Dalton watched them leave. When he turned to go

he found that Sheriff Blake was at his shoulder.

'You hear any of that?' Dalton asked.

'Enough,' Blake said.

Dalton sighed with relief. 'That mean you'll do something about it?'

'I will. But you won't.' He pointed back into the barn. 'You're staying to talk to everyone about this deal while I see Cliff Sinclair and ask him a few questions.'

'That's fine with me,' Dalton said raising his hands and backing away for a pace.

He watched Blake mount up and leave. Then he looked at the barn from where raised voices were sounding as the discussion gathered momentum.

He couldn't make out what everyone was saying, but amongst the commotion he clearly heard his own name being uttered several times.

Dalton moved to enter, but then with a shake of the head, he turned on his heels and walked away.

CHAPTER 3

A delegation was approaching.

After he'd ignored Sheriff Blake's advice and gone back home to await news, this didn't surprise Dalton, but the thought of debating the deal didn't fill him with enthusiasm.

For the last few hours Loren's death had dominated his thoughts. They had been friends for years and they had survived many scrapes together. When Dalton's wife Eliza had died last winter during a wave of illness that had swept through the community and decimated several families, he'd stood by him.

Now there was nothing left for him here but memories.

That thought resonated in his mind as he watched the variety of carts, wagons and horses draw to a halt. Then without preamble Wes Potter, one of the first to settle here, came forward, having clearly been elected to be the spokesman beforehand.

'You prepared to hear us out?' he asked.

'Sure,' Dalton said. 'As long as you're prepared to hear me out.'

Wes nodded. 'We talked and we want to take the money. Only you stand in our way.'

Dalton considered Wes's stance, noting he hadn't adopted an aggressive manner, and so he signified that he should take the seat beside him. Wes shook his head and so Dalton stood and joined him.

'Loren Steele died last night,' Dalton said, 'shot in his home while everything he'd built was torched. Does that concern you?'

'It does, but we have to move on. The money we'll get from—'

'From Cliff Sinclair, the man who killed him.'

Wes shook his head. 'Cliff had no reason to kill him. He was prepared to pay him the same as everyone else. We tried to talk you into accepting and if you didn't want to take the money, that was fine. But now we have to be unanimous. That changes everything.'

'And if I'm the only dissenter?'

'We hope that you won't be.' Wes considered him and lowered his tone. 'We all feel terrible about what happened to Eliza, but that just makes your determination to stay on here all the more confusing.'

Dalton firmed his jaw to avoid reacting and showing that Wes had made a good point.

'I'll think about it and let you have my decision by

sundown.' Dalton waited until Wes nodded before he continued. 'But that's provided you'll think about it and let me have your decision by then.'

'We've done that. We're accepting the offer.'

'I didn't mean the deal. I mean what you think about Cliff Sinclair. Blake is questioning him about Loren's death and someone will be under arrest soon.'

Dalton had chosen his words carefully as he was only sure that Blake would arrest Frank Kelley.

Wes opened his mouth to reply, then closed it with the thought unsaid. He headed over to join the others and gathered them around to convey his conversation.

The people frequently looked at him and the louder words that carried to him gave Dalton the impression they didn't reckon Cliff would get arrested. Finally Wes peeled away to give Dalton their decision, leaving the rest to return to their wagons and horses.

'We're still keen to take the offer,' he said, 'but we accept that might change if Blake arrests Cliff. That still won't mean he's guilty, but we will demand more time. If he doesn't arrest him. . . ?'

'Then as I said I'll let you have my decision by sundown.'

Wes glanced at the high summer sun then nodded and left to join everyone in leaving. Dalton watched them until they slipped out of view. He sat for a while, biding his time and waiting to see what happened.

He figured that Blake would come out to see him after he'd seen Cliff, but the afternoon passed without him arriving.

So in a pensive mood Dalton headed down to the river where he stood on a mound while he pondered. The broad sweep of the river carried on down past his home and the other homesteads before it was joined by two other rivers.

This meeting point had created a fertile area to the south, land that Cliff would be free to exploit if they left.

To the west was Cliff Sinclair's ranch, set a mile back from the river. Downriver was the bridge over Spinner's Gulch that had initiated the current crisis.

The railroad was moving over the river towards White Falls, this being the closest point the tracks could get to the gold mine that was high in the hills at Durando. The prosperity this would bring was sure to affect them all and many had thought of resettling in White Falls.

Then Cliff had decided to exploit the situation by expanding.

His offer to buy their land was a generous one that many ranchers in the same situation wouldn't have provided, but Dalton couldn't get over the uneasy feeling that something was amiss. Some offers are just too good to be true. . . .

A gunshot cracked, the sound distant but sharp.

Dalton snapped out of his reverie and looked upriver. A copse of trees was a mile away and the sound could have been the crack a tree makes when it falls, but it wasn't windy.

Another shot came from closer to, and this time there was no mistaking that it was shooting.

Dalton hurried back to his home. In short order he collected his Winchester, mounted up and rode towards the trees. Since the gunfire, he hadn't heard any further shots or untoward noises, but he rode on with his rifle sheath open.

He looked ahead for signs of trouble, but he reached the outlying trees without seeing anyone. On the outskirts of the copse he slowed. The first visible sign that something was amiss was a lone horse mooching towards him through the trees.

Dalton looked past the horse. A hundred yards into the trees there was a splash of colour. He couldn't tell what it was and so he dismounted cautiously.

With his rifle held low he headed on to investigate while moving from side to side to get an uninterrupted view between the trunks. When he finally saw the object ahead, it made him drop to his knees. A man was sitting propped up against a tree with a six-shooter on his lap, looking straight ahead.

Dalton watched him and although he appeared to

be sitting in a position where he could watch what was happening nearby he didn't register that he'd been seen.

Even so Dalton was cautious and he slipped backwards until he was out of sight. Then he skirted round to approach the tree from behind.

With vegetation matting the ground it was impossible to reach the tree silently and so when he was fifty yards away he didn't try to reduce the sound of his footfalls.

Bushes rustled and twigs snapped. He expected that at any moment the man would peer around the tree, but he reached it without being challenged then moved around to bring the man into view.

The man appeared to be looking at him, but he did so sightlessly. His vest front was blood-splattered with the stain spreading out from the heart.

Only a fortuitously placed low branch that had trapped an arm kept his lifeless body in a sitting position. His gun lay on his lap.

Dalton recalled that he had heard two shots. So he stood beside the body and looked where the dead man had last looked, then set off.

He'd managed only a few paces when he saw the other victim of this shoot-out, and this time it was someone he knew.

He broke into a run then skidded to a halt beside the form of Sheriff Blake. He was lying where he'd fallen face down in a bush.

Dalton placed a hand on his shoulder making Blake flinch then wave an arm weakly trying to shake him off. When this action failed he slapped the ground as he rooted around for his gun.

'It's me,' Dalton said. 'I'm here to help.'

Blake murmured his thanks and relaxed. Then, with Dalton's help, he shuffled round to lie on his back.

This let Dalton see he'd been shot low down in his side, a wound that wasn't necessarily lethal, but which would bring a slow, painful death if he didn't get him to help quickly.

Dalton moved to explore the wound, but Blake waved him away.

'The other?' he breathed.

'There's a dead man over there, if that's who you mean.'

'Yeah. He was the last of 'em.'

'Last of who?' Dalton asked, but Blake signified that he should help him get out of the bush before he spoke.

When Blake was sitting propped up against a tree facing the man who'd shot him, he barked out his story in terse bursts punctuated with sharp intakes of breath.

'You were right. Cliff Sinclair hired Frank Kelley. Frank killed Loren. Cliff's got a dozen more men back at his ranch. They tried to shoot me up. I got away. Two came after me. Got 'em both.' Blake winced as another bolt of pain racked through him. 'Get me moving.'

Dalton nodded, pleased despite the circumstances to hear confirmation that his suspicions were justified. He resisted the urge to ask more questions and wrapped an arm around his shoulders then manoeuvred him to his feet.

They stood until Blake murmured that he was ready. Then they moved off. It took a few stumbles followed by grunts of pain before they developed an effective walking rhythm.

When they reached the edge of the copse, Dalton left Blake leaning against a tree then rounded up the dead man's horse. Getting Blake on to it proved to be a difficult task.

In the end he had to let the sheriff sit on his shoulders and he stood up. But once Blake was mounted, he grunted that he felt better, even if the beads of sweat on his forehead and his drawn expression suggested he was exaggerating.

At a slow trot they rode on. Dalton pressed Blake for more details of what had happened, mainly to distract him from the pain, but Blake merely grunted uncommitted answers as he concentrated on keeping himself upright.

They took the shortest route to the river, then skirted along the bank. Dalton kept a lookout for anyone else following them, but when he saw trouble it came from an unexpected direction.

Beyond a small rise, smoke was spiralling up into the late afternoon sky, and it was coming from the direction of his house.

CHAPTER 4

After making sure that Sheriff Blake didn't mind being left alone, Dalton hurried his horse back along the river. He faced the smoke, which was getting denser with every passing moment.

His house was behind a rise and when he crested it, the sight ahead made him draw back on the reins. His house was ablaze, the flames bright and angry. People were riding towards the house, but they were some distance away and already the battle to save it would be futile.

What drew Dalton's attention next were the ten riders heading away from the house. They had reached the bottom of the rise and although they were 200 yards away, Dalton saw that Frank Kelley was riding up front.

Dalton hurried out of sight before he could be seen then rode back down to the river. Every few paces he looked back at the black smoke, the sight giving him a hollow and futile feeling in his guts. When he caught up with Blake, he agreed that these men were probably the ones who had attacked him at Cliff's ranch.

'Clearly they've decided to end this quickly,' Blake said.

'We need to hole up and plan how we'll stop them.'

Blake looked at him with a teeth-gritted expression that said he doubted he could help. But he gripped the reins with a determined snap of the wrist and headed on at a fast trot.

Dalton followed on behind letting Blake dictate the pace he could manage while staying on lookout for the riders. They maintained a fair pace, although the riders could easily better it. But to Dalton's relief the men didn't ride into view.

When they reached the first of the rivers that flowed into the main river Dalton thought that by now they should have appeared, but on the other hand they might not have seen him.

As the smoke rippled skyward they skirted the river, but before they reached the shallow area where it could be forded, Frank Kelley and his men appeared, riding towards them having skirted around the rise in the opposite direction.

They rode towards them at a confident pace. Blake was already rolling in the saddle. He would struggle to maintain their pace for long even if they could cross the river first.

'We won't hole up,' Dalton said, putting a positive outlook on their difficult situation. 'We'll double-back to Two Forks.'

Blake sat tall, winced, then rubbed a rueful hand around his wound. He drew the hand away and considered the bright blood, then wiped it on his jacket.

'We'll never make it past them,' he said. 'It has to be White Falls.'

'We'll never reach there.'

Blake gave him a long stare, then lowered his voice.

'One of us won't.'

'Forget that talk,' Dalton said.

'I can't hold on no longer. The homesteaders will be safe if they accept Cliff's terms. But you'll get what Loren got. You need to tell Deputy Lawton the full story.'

This was a long speech for the wounded lawman to make and when Dalton started to respond, he raised a hand and fixed him with a pained glare, showing it'd taken a lot out of him.

Dalton noted that the men were now urging their horses on to meet them at a gallop. He gripped the reins tightly, determined to ignore the order, but then with a slap of a fist against his thigh he moved his horse to the side and galloped away into the water, leaving Blake behind.

While traversing the river he resisted the urge to

look back, but when he'd come out on the other side he glanced over his shoulder. Blake hadn't moved. He was facing the riders, who were advancing on him with steady menace.

Dalton turned away. Then, after murmuring his hopes that the sheriff would prevail despite the odds, he concentrated on riding fast and putting distance between himself and Frank. He'd reached the first bend in the river when a gunshot peeled out.

This heralded a sudden burst of gunfire, then silence.

Dalton didn't look back, keeping his thoughts away from dwelling on what had happened to Blake. He had managed only another mile when a bend in the river let him see to his side. Frank Kelley and his men were on his tail. Their numbers didn't appear to have been diminished.

He faced downriver and rode on.

As the afternoon turned to twilit gloom he tried to get ahead of his pursuers, but the men were relentless. They rode beside the river, never letting him out their sight.

Neither did they make a move to overwhelm him, presumably because they were achieving what they wanted to by shepherding him away from Two Forks. Downriver there were no settlements other than the town of White Falls, and the railroad workers' camps on the advancing tracks and at Spinner's Gulch.

As he couldn't reach either without a rest Dalton

looked for somewhere to hole up. One place sprang to mind, a location he'd seen on one of his infrequent trips downriver with Loren.

So at a shallow point he forded the river, reaching the other side as his pursuers ventured into the water, then headed off across country.

The terrain rose towards his destination of a cutting a mile on where the railroad had blasted through a hill so that they could have a relatively straight and flat route to Spinner's Gulch. Within the cutting there were ledges and hollows and on one occasion he and Loren had spent the night there sheltering from the wind.

The pursuers must have known there were potential hiding places ahead as for the first time they speeded up. As the edge of the cutting came into view a half mile on, appearing as a straight, dark slash across the land with the sheer sides dropping away from him, they inexorably closed in on him.

Dalton searched for a burst of speed from his sweat-licked mount. This worked for a few hundred yards, but the long unexpected journey was proving to be too much of a strain. Every time he looked back the riders were closer: seventy yards, fifty, thirty. . . . At twenty yards they spread out seeking to round him up. And the top of the rise was still fifty yards away.

A gunshot tore out, heralding a volley of shots. All were thankfully high but when he looked back several riders were firming their gun arms so clearly the shots hadn't been warnings.

The next volley exploded and this time with a cry of almost human pain his horse whinnied. A bullet had ripped into her flank. The head dropped, legs crossed and folded. Then Dalton was tossed out of the saddle as his horse stumbled to its knees.

Dalton just had enough time to prepare himself. He tucked himself up and hit the ground on his side then rolled.

Experience told him that although there was no foolproof way of avoiding serious injury, the best option was to relax and not throw out a hand to try to cushion his fall. The rest was down to luck.

That luck held when he rolled to a standstill and found that he could flex his limbs without undue pain.

He glanced at his mount, lying twitching in its death-throws, but he didn't have enough time to help her as the pursuers were closing in from three sides. Neither did he have the time to fetch his rifle.

So he did the only thing he could do. He got to his feet and ran to the cutting even though all he could see was the sheer drop down to the rail track.

He didn't know how far away the recesses that he'd found were. When he reached the edge and was confronted with the darkness of the cutting below, its bottom shrouded in the gathering gloom, he was sure that he'd never be able to find them.

Coming from his right a whistle from an

approaching train shrilled in the evening air. He looked along the cutting until he saw the long line of cars struggling up the slight incline several hundred yards away.

Despite being unable to see the bottom he was sure if he attempted the leap, he would shatter every bone in his body. So he turned to face his pursuers, finding that the riders had stopped and that they had fanned out in a semicircle to block his escape paths.

'You going to tell me what this is about?' he said to give himself time to think of a plan rather than because he thought they might answer.

Frank nudged his horse on to be ahead of the others.

'Nope,' he said. 'You get the same explanation as Sheriff Blake got.'

As one his men raised their guns to sight him.

'Wait!' Dalton shouted, backing away for another pace to the edge. This let him see down into the cutting where the engine was drawing level with him. It was ferrying several open loads, but he couldn't tell what they were.

'Why?' Frank said in a clipped tone.

'Because. . . .' Dalton waved his hands as he struggled to find a response that would keep him safe for a few more moments. 'Because I didn't think clearly about Cliff Sinclair's offer. Maybe I'll take it, after all.'

The engine rattled as it passed below him, forcing

Frank to raise his voice.

'The rest had more sense and took the money. You had your chance, but you chose death.'

Frank looked at his men in a determined manner that said he'd finished talking and so Dalton glanced down at the train. He could see the long lengths it was carrying and in the poor light they could be either rail tracks or planks. Both were probably equally unlikely to cushion his fall but he figured he didn't have much of a choice.

'Obliged you heard me out,' Dalton said. He glared at Frank Kelley, committing his anger about Loren's murder to memory. Then he pointed a firm finger at him and raised his voice. 'But somehow I will make you pay.'

The taunt made Frank laugh, but that had been the result Dalton had hoped for. With the distraction buying him more time, he spun on his heels. He ran the three paces to the edge and launched himself into space.

Gunfire tore out, blasting through the air above his head. All of it missed, but gunfire was the least of Dalton's worries as he hurtled down towards his uncertain fate below.

The wind whipped by as he plummeted through the darkness and he looked down seeking a clue as to what he'd land on, but quicker than he expected the dark mass of the train's load loomed closer.

He crashed down on solid lengths, the reek of

pine surrounding him and at least telling him he'd landed on wood. Then he kept going downwards as his momentum made him snap through several planks and bury him between others.

When he came to a halt, he was buried up to the shoulders in wood. It trapped him on all sides, but apart from his legs feeling jarred, he reckoned the drop had been shorter than he'd feared and he'd avoided any broken limbs.

He ducked down then took stock of his situation.

The wood was trapping him in place and he would probably struggle to free himself when he tried to get out. With the cutting carrying on for several miles it would be some time before Frank managed to get down to meet the train. Then, if he remained hidden, Frank might assume that either he'd fallen to his death or he'd tried to escape in the dark. So for now, he decided he'd settle for going where the train was heading.

He rested in his wooden prison until he was sure that the immediate danger of being shot at from above had passed. Then he began the process of freeing his limbs.

One arm was trapped at his side, but he could move the other. So he walked his hand down his side to grip his right leg. Then he strained to raise it from the planks that were encasing it.

At first he couldn't move the leg, but when his wriggling dislodged other planks, he was able to raise it slightly. Heartened by his success he tried to move his left leg.

A heavy thud sounded and the planks shifted position. For one terrible moment Dalton couldn't breathe and his legs were dragged in two directions at once. But then the wood settled giving him enough leeway to gasp in air.

The sudden movement added urgency to his need to free himself from the wood, but then he found out the reason for the shift. Someone had jumped down and like him he was buried in the heaps of wood.

Dalton peered into the darkness. He couldn't see where the other man had landed. He craned his neck, but then a grunt sounded behind him. Someone wrapped an arm around his neck and tugged.

The force slammed his shoulders against the wood behind him then made his head pivot backwards until it rested on the wood. His posture was so taut it closed his windpipe.

He gulped, only a thin stream of air reaching his lungs. In desperation he waved his arms, but trapped within the planks he couldn't stretch his arms back far enough to reach his assailant. Grunting sounded as the man bore down on him, but with him straining more, he dragged Dalton backwards.

The different angle closed off the thin stream of air, but it also drew Dalton's body out of the vice-like grip of the planks. With him able to move, Dalton thrust his arms backwards and this time he brushed the man's head.

He wasn't able to co-ordinate his hands, but after three frantic lunges that his assailant jerked away from, he grabbed the man's ear with one hand and tugged, making him bleat. And a poke with the other hand jabbed a finger into something wet and which from the cry of pain that went up, must have been an eye.

The pressure around his throat fell away. Dalton gasped in air, but he forced himself to continue to fight back and press home his advantage. He twisted then levered himself out of the chasm of wood into which he'd fallen to roll out on to the top.

Below him the man was standing trapped between planks in the same way that Dalton had been earlier, but even if his legs were buried, he was armed. He glared up at Dalton with one eyed closed then swung his six-shooter round to aim it up at him.

On his knees Dalton lunged and grabbed the man's wrist, but he still loosed off a wild skyward shot. Then he concentrated on bringing the arm down towards Dalton's head, while Dalton strained to turn it towards the man's chest.

The gun wavered back and forth as both men strained for supremacy. Then slowly his assailant got the upper hand. Being trapped within the planks gave him traction while Dalton couldn't find purchase on the top of the wood. Inexorably he was shoved backwards.

He could do nothing to stop the gun closing in on him while the gunman grinned as he anticipated firing the moment he had Dalton in his sights.

Dalton twisted away to avoid the advancing gun, but that only encouraged his assailant to redouble his efforts. The gun speeded its approach. It edged past his shoulder then nuzzled beside his neck. Dalton strained to move himself away and bought himself a few more inches.

Eager to plant a bullet in him, his assailant fired. The deafening explosion was close to Dalton's ear making him flinch. Momentarily he lost his grip on the gun. The release of pressure made the gun swing wildly past Dalton's body and slam down on the plank.

Before the man could raise the weapon Dalton thrust his knee forward and trapped his wrist against the wood. Then he followed through with a round-armed punch to the man's face that knocked his head back.

With the gun-toter being trapped, Dalton aimed another flailing punch at him, but the man ducked beneath it before coming up with a straight-armed shove that toppled Dalton and sent him sprawling.

Loose planks skidded beneath his feet as he fell backwards. He back-pedalled seeking purchase but he only succeeded in dislodging more planks from underfoot. Worse, the man was raising himself from his wooden prison with his gun held high.

Dalton couldn't see why the previously immobile planks now had the solidity of sand, although he consoled himself with the observation that the gunman was having as much trouble as he was in righting himself. Then Dalton saw what had happened.

When his assailant had fired he'd missed his target and instead he'd winged one of the ropes that were holding the load in place. That rope was fluttering free and the planks were redistributing themselves.

The man hadn't seen this. He gave up trying to get out and instead he centred his gun in on Dalton. With a scrambling kick Dalton tried to get away, but then with a grinding of timbers the outermost two columns of wood peeled away from the bulk and crashed down to the ground below.

The noise made the man look to the side just as another column gave way. He fired a speculative wild shot. Then planks cascaded to the ground and an undulating tide of wooden chaos carried him away.

When he'd disappeared from view, planks continued to slide, but now with around a third of the bulk having slipped away the remainder found a natural level on the speeding train.

Dalton stayed still until he was sure he wouldn't slip away after the man. Then he edged along the planks and made his way on to the top of the load on the next car where he lay on his chest.

The fallen wood was now disappearing into the darkness as the train emerged from the cutting. The darkened plains were on either side. Ahead there were small faint lights.

On his belly he watched them, wondering if he were seeing after-images brought on by the strain of the fight. Then in a change of perspective he saw that the lights were bright but far away. To add a further hint of what they were, the train brakes screeched as the engine slowed. It was the end of the line.

Closer to, Dalton saw the campfires burning amidst the sprawling gang of workers who were building the tracks on towards the bridge at Spinner's Gulch.

Dalton settled down, judging that for now being amongst people was his safest option. He enjoyed watching the sprawl of tents in this effectively mobile town open up to him.

By the time he was able to identify individuals the train had slowed to a crawl as it aimed to stop a hundred yards away from the end of the tracks.

Accordingly, several people walked on to meet the train. Dalton moved to climb down and meet them, but then he saw who was in the leading group.

Frank Kelley was walking towards him, and the other men who had chased him were following on behind.

CHAPTER 5

Dalton slid backwards along the top of the planks like a snake, seeking to distance himself from the advancing Frank while he thought out a plan to escape.

He had a spot of luck when the railroad men amongst the approaching group saw the chaotic jumble of planks and hurried past Frank to inspect the damage. With the milling people giving him some cover Dalton continued to slide away.

Keeping his profile low, he slipped down to stand on the edge of the car. Having checked that everyone was approaching along one side of the train, he jumped down to the ground on the other.

'When I find out who didn't tie these planks down properly,' a loud, official sounding voice said, 'I'll be heading back down the line to bang some heads together.'

'I'll get a wagon,' a softer voice said, 'and find them.'

Dalton peered beneath the cars. Beyond the jumble of planks hanging off the side of the car five men were glaring at the mess.

Frank and his group stood further back. Frank was gesturing. Then three men moved to go around the engine to investigate the other side. Dalton slipped between the two cars to keep out of sight.

'The wood could be a hundred miles away.'

Several planks moved as the softer speaker raised himself to look on the car.

'There's still plenty of wood on here. If the rest had come lose a hundred miles back they'd have all shaken loose by now.'

A non-committed grunt sounded that confirmed this was a good point while not slackening his authority by being supportive.

'Then stop standing around and find it.'

Dalton leaned down. Frank's group was one car away, so he sought a place to hide, but other than crawling beneath the train he couldn't see an option. Worse, one of the men leaned down to look underneath and despite the shadows Dalton felt sure he would have seen him.

Still bent over Dalton edged into the middle of the tracks, torn between which escape route would give him the best chance of success.

'I judge that around a third slipped off,' the subordinate continued. 'That's not—'

'I don't care how much slipped off. I want it back, and I don't want you wasting half the night searching for it.'

'Then we'll work out how much we're looking for and leave.'

Two men walked around the side of the car to appraise the displaced wood.

The man who hadn't spoken had his gaze set on the wood, but the talkative man looked at Dalton. Behind him other men swung into view, but they were all sloping along with the air of workers who'd had a tiring day and weren't relishing this extension to their duties.

Dalton turned from the man to look under the train at Frank's men advancing on either side while he picked his moment to run.

A rustling sounded behind him and something encased him. He tried to throw it off, but then he found that a thick and long coat had been wrapped around his shoulders.

He turned to find its former owner winking at him. Then he placed a hand on Dalton's back and ushered him away from the cars and into full view.

'This is sure to be a long journey,' he announced in a chatty manner, as if they were old friends, 'but I say that the sooner we get there, the sooner we get back.'

Dalton drew down the brim of his hat and ignored

Frank and the approaching men, judging that his new friend might be correct that the best place to hide could be in full view.

'Yeah,' he grunted, attempting a disguised tone of voice, 'we get all the roughest job, but do we ever complain?'

'We sure don't. You never hear a word of complaint from our lips. They give us a task. We do it without saying nothing.'

The worker continued to prattle but they'd now drawn level with Frank. Dalton paid him only scant attention, and luckily Frank ignored the railroad workers and continued to glare along the length of the train while his men searched for him. Then Dalton moved past.

Dalton resisted the urge to look back and so ruin his disguise. But when the rest of the wood detail hurried on to catch up with them, he couldn't resist asking the obvious question.

'Why?' he said from the corner of his mouth.

'Any enemy of Frank Kelley is a friend of mine.' His new friend glanced back then gave an encouraging nod. 'But once you're out of sight, I want that coat back.'

Dalton nodded then headed on while hoping Frank didn't notice the deception.

He learnt that the man who had helped him was Booth Hughes. He'd been discussing the fallen wood with Victor McCoy, who oversaw the bridge building.

The wood was to be used there and its lateness had worsened his temperament, which was brusque at the best of times.

When they reached the end of the tracks, Dalton mingled in with the other workers who had gathered to await instructions. Only then did he look back.

He was pleased to see that Frank and his men were still working their way around the train looking for him. Victor McCoy was heading back towards them.

When he arrived, he wasted no time in haranguing Booth.

'Why are you still here?' he demanded. 'I need that wood.'

'We're leaving,' Booth said. He gestured to the men who would go with him, including Dalton, then moved towards the nearest wagon.

Dalton adopted the workers' sloping posture and followed, but his route took him past Victor.

The men went by him in a line, but when Dalton passed by, Victor slapped a hand on his shoulder, halting him. Then, without saying a word, he dragged the coat off and threw it to Booth.

'You're not going with them,' he said.

'I'm a good worker,' Dalton murmured, still trying to maintain his disguise. 'I'm sure we can find the missing wood.'

Victor smiled. 'I'm sure you can, but I have a more important task for you.'

*

Dalton's first sight of the bridge impressed him.

He had travelled downriver with Loren when the work had first started, but in the intervening months the structure had grown faster than he'd expected.

Sitting with him on the front of the wood-laden wagon were two other workers, neither of whom had spoken to him and neither of whom had shown any sign of knowing that he didn't work for the railroad.

Victor hadn't told him why he'd let him go to the bridge, but Dalton was glad he had. Frank had sent one of his men with Booth's detail and his disguise would probably have been uncovered quickly.

The driver drew up the wagon close to the edge of the gulch and workers emerged from the gloom to begin unloading the planks. Dalton helped out, losing himself in the physical work, but it also gave him time to think.

Victor hadn't accompanied the wagons so he wouldn't be getting an explanation any time soon. And he was unsure whether he needed one. Perhaps Victor, like Booth, had helped him to spite Frank Kelley, who was clearly more infamous than just being a gun-toter who Cliff Sinclair had hired to kill Loren Steele.

As Dalton helped unload the wood, he considered how he could carry out Blake's last instructions of finding Deputy Lawton.

As Frank had followed him here after killing Sheriff Blake, he wouldn't have had enough time to attack the other homesteaders. But clearly they were in danger and he needed to act before the deadline for them to accept Cliff Sinclair's deal expired in two days.

He didn't welcome the long walk to White Falls, and he hadn't thought of a way to get a horse beyond just stealing one when a final wagon arrived with the reclaimed wood.

It lined up behind the unloaded wagons. Booth was riding up front. Victor had come with him and he started berating anyone who strayed close enough with complaints about their tardiness.

His arrival instigated a greater sense of urgency and more workers appeared to complete the job. When everyone was bustling to his satisfaction Victor caught Dalton's eye and gave a brief head flick that signified where they would talk.

Accordingly, Dalton headed to the edge of the gulch where in the shadow of an archway Victor joined him.

'Who are you?' he asked without preamble.

'I'm Dalton. I live in Two Forks.'

'Why is Frank Kelley after you?'

'It's a long story, but in brief Cliff Sinclair is buying up the homesteaders' land in Two Forks. He hired Frank to kill anyone who wouldn't accept his deal. That included me and so I ran.'

Dalton had intended to provide more details, but Victor was giving him odd looks that suggested he knew some of these details but from a different perspective.

'So you want to stay out of Frank's way and move on?' he asked with an odd inflection that warned Dalton of an impending problem.

'I do,' he said cautiously, 'and I'm grateful that you didn't tell Frank about me.'

'I didn't talk, but it's yet to be decided if I'll continue to keep quiet.'

'What do you mean?' Dalton snapped.

Victor shot him a narrowed-eyed glare that said he wouldn't accept further outbursts, then turned Dalton to face the bridge.

'Frank Kelley has influence beyond Two Forks. My task is to complete this bridge before the tracks arrive, except the work is going slowly, the deadline is getting tighter, and I don't know why.'

'I'm sorry to hear that, but I don't see what that has got to do with Frank, or me.'

'You will do.' Victor pointed at three men who were eyeing the operations with surly disinterest. 'See them?'

'Sure.'

Victor turned back to the bridge.

'Then don't let them notice that you've seen them. They're with Frank: Seth Elliott, Thomas Jeffries and Caleb Scarron. Since they arrived the workers have been edgy and their work's been shoddy. Worse, if I don't pay Frank, they'll make sure the bridge isn't completed on time.'

'And you're not paying?'

'Never. But what worries me more is whether he has other men here that I don't know about. So I need to know if they're alone and what mischief they're planning.'

Dalton narrowed his eyes. 'And you want me to find out?'

Victor smiled. 'When I saw that Frank Kelley was looking for you I knew you were the right man for the job.'

'And if I don't?'

'I'll curry favour with Frank by telling him where you are.'

Dalton rubbed his chin. He needed to move on to White Falls, but he also wanted vengeance. Clearly Frank had wormed his way into the bridge building as well as working for Cliff. So completing Victor's task would help him start fighting back against Frank.

'Then,' he said, 'I reckon I'll be making some new friends.'

Victor nodded. He looked at his feet and when he looked up his expression was thunderous. He paced up to Dalton then pushed him.

'Where did you come from?' he demanded.

'I agreed to do—'

'I said,' Victor muttered, speaking over his objection, 'who paid you to cut the ropes on the train and ruin that lumber load?'

Dalton was about to object again, but Victor didn't give him a chance to speak and a second firm shove sent him sprawling. On the ground he glared up at Victor, but then he saw that their conversation had gathered interest. Seth Elliott was heading closer.

Dalton gave a brief nod, acknowledging what Victor was doing, then got to his feet and adopted a truculent stance.

'I don't have to explain nothing to you,' he shouted while gesturing at Victor. 'With the wages you pay, I reckon I'll leave.'

'Then go before I kick you off the bridge.'

Dalton paced up to Victor with his fists bunched and looking as if he'd knock him over, but after glaring at him for several moments he waved a dismissive hand and paced off back to the wagons.

Seth was standing in his way considering their argument with interest, but maintaining his disguise of being a disgruntled worker Dalton stopped before him then looked him up and down, sneering.

'What you looking at?' he demanded.

'I wanted to speak to Victor,' Seth said with an amused smile on his lips. 'You finished?'

'You're welcome to him.'

Dalton barged past Seth then walked on to rejoin the wagons. He avoided looking at Seth and Victor, but when he'd helped unload another wagon he got the opportunity to look around.

Seth and his men were still not helping with the work, but they were watching him and whispering to each other.

CHAPTER 6

'Get to work,' Oliver Riley demanded, kicking Dalton's legs to make him stand up.

Oliver was in charge of the detail on which Victor had placed him. Booth had claimed that Oliver was a fair man, but Dalton had a role to play and Thomas, one of Seth's two known associates, was with his detail.

As he didn't want to appear too eager by talking to him first, he'd adopted a surly attitude in the hope that Thomas would come to him. When they'd set off for work he'd dallied at the back. Then he'd worked slowly during the morning and after a short break he was ensuring he was the last to get up.

'Yeah, yeah,' Dalton murmured. 'I heard you the first time.'

He stood slowly, dusted down his pants, then sloped off to join the others on the bridge.

Oliver eyed him with irritation and when he

joined Booth, so did his new friend.

'The work here is hard,' Booth said, 'but there's nothing else available. Oliver will get rid of you if you don't start behaving.'

Dalton gritted his teeth to avoid showing how guilty he felt at his deception.

'I'll do my fair share,' he said, 'but I'm not getting myself noticed or I could end up chasing after wood that's fallen off a train.'

Booth accepted his excuse with a rueful smile and so they got started on the afternoon's work.

The detail had the task of raising a pile of rocks from the bottom of the gulch that was to be used to make a raised area for the tracks on the approach to the bridge. A four-man team attached baskets to a pulley that dangled over the edge and loaded them. Then Booth and Dalton raised the baskets.

Booth ensured the rope moved smoothly and safely while Dalton supervised the bow-backed bay that circled around a winch and so raised the rope. They got to rest while the team at the top moved the rocks aside. Then they repeated the process.

Oliver had two groups working on either side of the bridge and he paced back and forth cajoling whichever team was working the slowest. Whenever he was with the other group everyone relaxed and talked more.

So Dalton wasn't surprised when in mid-afternoon Thomas wandered over to join him. He watched him walking the horse round, then caught his eye.

'You're right to ignore Oliver,' Thomas said. 'He's a fool.'

'I'd like to see him loading up this ballast,' Dalton said, getting into the spirit of the required conversation.

'Yeah. I'd dump him in a basket.' Thomas mimed placing him on a large pile. Then he dropped his hand. 'Then I'd make this nag gallop and watch him go shooting up the gulch a-screaming and a-hollering. Now that sure would be a sight.'

'It's a great thought, but it'd be almost as much fun as seeing this horse galloping.' Dalton laughed then glanced at the docile horse lumbering its way round. 'You couldn't make it move fast even if you set its tail on fire.'

'Not its tail,' Thomas said while considering him with a malicious gleam in his eye. He looked around to check that nobody was close then reached into his pocket and passed him a potato. 'The next time Oliver is with the other group, wait until the load is about to come up. Then feed it that potato and stand back to enjoy what happens next.'

Dalton quickly pocketed the potato. 'And what will happen?'

'It'll gulp it down, but then its guts will start blazing and it'll bolt. The rope will go hurtling round and bring the ballast up so fast it'll break the winch and send the whole load crashing down. With any luck it'll flatten a few men below.'

Dalton winced, but luckily Thomas was looking elsewhere while he described his plan.

'Just give the word,' he said, deciding that anything else wouldn't be appropriate.

'Wait until I give the signal by taking off my hat to mop my brow. Then do it.'

Thomas gave him a firm look to which Dalton nodded. Then Thomas returned to his place leaving Dalton to wonder how he could carry out a plan that would get him closer to Seth without endangering everyone's lives.

For the next hour he smirked whenever Thomas caught his eye, but Oliver spent most of the time with them so he could berate them every few minutes about how they were the slowest group of the two. When he did leave them the basket was on its way up and so it was too late to carry out the plan.

Thomas still caught his eye with a significant look that said their time would come if they were patient.

Fifteen minutes later Oliver still hadn't returned and so while the next pile of ballast was being loaded below, Dalton joined Booth. He checked that Thomas wasn't close then leaned towards him.

'When I shout out,' Dalton said from the corner of his mouth, 'don't try to stop the winch.'

'What do you—?'

'And make sure everybody below gets out of the way.'

Booth opened his mouth to continue asking questions, but then his gaze darted to Thomas before he looked back at Dalton. He curled his upper lip in disgust.

'I should have let Frank Kelley find you,' he said, then went to stand on his own.

Dalton watched him leave, wishing he could explain himself, but he'd done as much as he could without drawing suspicion upon himself. He went back to the old horse and waited for the ballast to be loaded up.

When the strain had been taken and the load was swinging out over the gulch, Thomas looked around to check that nobody was paying Dalton any attention. Then he removed his hat to mop his brow while looking over the side, deliberately ignoring him.

Dalton reached into his pocket, but when he withdrew his hand it was empty. He still patted the horse and let it nuzzle him before they embarked on a steady circle.

On completing a circle, Thomas caught his eye and Dalton nodded. Thomas smirked and while rubbing his hands with suppressed glee he stood back to await developments.

Dalton kept an eye on the pulley from the corner of his eye judging the moment when he could act safely. But the workers were shouting directions from down below and he judged that as usual they were standing close by so they could direct operations.

If he acted, it would need a stroke of luck for nobody to get badly hurt. So he continued to lead the horse around and when the ballast reached the top he sought out Thomas and shrugged.

Thomas glared at the horse then at the ballast before he started unloading it. Dalton waited until the empty basket was about to be thrown down then slipped the potato out of his pocket and let the horse eat it. Then as always he wandered over to the pulley.

Despite nothing having happened Booth still looked at him with disgust. Dalton didn't retort and instead looked at the horse with a bemused expression.

From the corner of his eye he saw that Thomas was also looking bemused, but that bemusement ended when an aggrieved neigh sounded. Then the horse bustled against its winch rope. It surged one way then the other, shaking its mangy mane.

The commotion caught everyone's attention and others joined Dalton in rushing over to calm the horse, but nobody dared to stray close to its hoofs. Then, with a kick of its heels it bounded off, toppling the winch and dragging the rope behind it with the pulley attached.

Cries and hoots went up from the workers as they dodged out of the way of the galloping horse and trailing accompaniments. By the time Oliver hurried over to survey the scene, the winch mechanism had been destroyed, although Dalton had timed the spooking of the horse well as the basket hadn't been loaded and so nobody had been hurt.

This didn't please Oliver. It would take time to get the winch running and it was time they couldn't afford to lose. Someone had to take the blame and that man was Dalton.

'I don't know what happened,' Dalton said, spreading his hands while Oliver glowered at him. 'One minute the horse was lumbering around and then something must have spooked it as it shot off.'

'It did, didn't it?' Oliver said with deliberate slowness, as if he already knew why. Behind him Thomas was avoiding looking their way, although he was smirking at the successful result.

'I'll fetch the horse,' Dalton offered, 'and then we'll get the winch working again.'

'You will. All the ballast gets moved today even if you have to drag every rock up here yourself.'

With that statement of intent Oliver directed Booth to join Dalton in finding the horse, but with a surly grunt Booth refused. He suggested Thomas should go instead. This comment made Oliver nod knowingly.

Thomas didn't show that he'd noticed this exchange and as they trooped away after the fleeing horse, he was in good spirits.

'That horse must be even more thick-skinned than I thought,' he said. 'I thought it'd never get spooked.'

'I know. Perhaps I should feed it two potatoes the next time.'

Thomas laughed. 'That's a fine idea, but there can't be a next time. Oliver will get too suspicious.'

'A pity. That's the most fun I've had since I got here.'

As they moved beyond the circle of workers around the bridge, they caught their first sight of the horse ahead, now mooching around and returning to its normal docile state.

Dalton stayed quiet, deciding not to push his luck by appearing too eager to cause mayhem. That turned out to be the right decision when Thomas leaned towards him.

'If you're minded,' he said, 'there's plenty more we can do.'

'Such as?'

'We're finishing what we started.' Thomas stopped and looked around to check nobody was near. 'We're going to blow up the bridge and send Oliver and Victor and all the rest to hell.'

CHAPTER 7

'I know what they're planning,' Dalton whispered.

'You did well,' Victor whispered back. 'What is it?'

'They're blowing up the bridge.'

This revelation shocked Victor into silence.

It was now night. The detail had repaired the winch and pulley, but they hadn't managed to raise all the ballast. They would be starting work early tomorrow so that they could catch up.

With their evening meal eaten, the exhausted workers hadn't had the energy for the chatter and card games that apparently usually filled the evening. Most of the men had retired to the tents, but with nobody wanting to talk to Dalton after his role in the accident, he'd gone to sit alone beside the bridge.

Despite the urgency of seeing Victor, Dalton had waited until Victor found him.

'When?' Victor murmured when he at last found his voice.

'I don't know yet. But they want me to have a role in it.'

'Then find out all you can before it's too late.'

'I've done what you asked and the deadline for the Two Forks folk to accept Cliff Sinclair's deal expires at sundown tomorrow. I have to leave.'

This comment made Victor relax his posture and he swung round to sit beside Dalton.

'Go to the tents.' Victor pointed then patted him on the back. 'It'll put your mind at rest.'

Dalton asked for an explanation, but Victor said nothing else and with them already having pushed their luck with the length of their meeting, Dalton left.

The tents he'd been directed to were occupied by the workers who laid the trusses for the bridge. He hadn't spoken to any of them, so he wasn't sure who or what he needed to see there, but he didn't have to look far.

The answer found him.

'Dalton,' a familiar voice said. 'I wondered where you'd gone.'

Dalton turned to see Wes Potter coming out of the shadows, a man who he'd last seen when he'd tried to talk him into accepting Cliff Sinclair's deal yesterday, a time that now felt an age away.

'It's good to see you alive,' Dalton said hurrying over to him.

The men shook hands and exchanged pleasantries with no sign of their previous friction resurfacing. Wes was the first to bring up the subject that concerned Dalton.

'I was sorry about what happened to your house,' he said, 'but we didn't find out whether you still got the money.'

'Of course I didn't,' Dalton snapped.

Wes frowned. 'That's a pity. The rest of us did.'

This comment rendered Dalton speechless. He had hoped everyone would get out of what he had thought was an increasingly desperate situation, but he'd never once considered that Cliff would make good his offer.

'And he let you all leave?' he said finally.

'As I said he would. You shouldn't have doubted him.'

'There has to be a catch. Did Frank Kelley return?'

'He didn't, but then again. . . .' Wes sighed then moved on to take a steady walk away from the tents. 'We went to see Cliff together. He said everything that had happened recently was a misunderstanding and he had nothing to do with Loren's death. He paid us before the deadline.'

'And the money provided all the answers you needed?' Dalton waited for an answer but Wes's shame-faced look suggested he was right. 'And what about Sheriff Blake?'

'We didn't see him after he went to see Cliff.'

'You wouldn't. Frank Kelley and his men shot

66

him to hell.'

Wes stopped and kicked at the dirt. 'I didn't know that and I don't know why all those strange things happened back at Two Forks, but perhaps that means we were right to move on. And that includes you, even if you didn't get the money.'

Dalton shook his head. 'It was never about the money. Frank Kelley killed my friend Loren and then Sheriff Blake saved my life before Frank shot him up. I can't let this rest.'

'Then I wish you luck.' Wes bit his lip acknowledging that he felt guilty about not offering to help. 'But when this is over, seek me out in White Falls.'

'So you're not here to work?'

'No.' Wes looked around nervously to check nobody was close. 'I've got Cliff's money on me and there's too many light-fingered men here. I'll head to White Falls and see what a man with money can do for himself in a booming town. I reckon most of the others will do that too.'

'When you get there, tell Deputy Lawton what happened to Blake.'

'I'll do that.'

'And then, despite everything, I hope it works out well for you.'

Wes frowned, showing he was still rooting around for something he could do or say that would help Dalton. Then he brightened.

'I hope to set myself up in business, but it's not

right that you came out of it with nothing. Seek me out and I'll give you a place to rest up and, well, a share in whatever business I set up, if you're minded.'

Dalton smiled. 'I just hope I live for long enough to take you up on that offer.'

As the work detail trooped off to the winch in the dark, nobody talked to Dalton. Oliver had kicked everyone awake at an early hour to catch up with the work they'd failed to do yesterday, reminding everyone of his part in the disaster.

Dalton was allocated the hardest task of unloading the baskets from the pulley. Although nobody had volunteered to do this task yesterday, Thomas took up a position beside him.

They worked silently, but when they had their first break as the empty basket was lowered, he signified they should walk away from the others to talk.

'You ready?' Thomas asked.

'When you want my help,' Dalton said, 'just tell me.'

'Good. We should get this job done before sun-up. So nobody will be around to see what we do then.'

Dalton had expected that the attempt to blow up the bridge would be a long-term plan involving days of preparation in which he would have ample time to warn Victor. He hadn't considered it would be within the hour.

He shook his shock away and said the only thing he could say.

'Just give the word,' he said. Then before anyone noted them talking he headed back to the pulley to await the next basket.

Thomas said no more about their plans and so Dalton could do nothing but continue to work while looking out for signs of life from the tents so he could get a message to Victor.

Working steadily they winched the eight outstanding loads to the top. No others workers appeared and as time passed Dalton began to think nobody would and it'd be left to him to foil this plot.

The arc of light was expanding on the eastern horizon when Oliver signified that they'd now caught up with where they should be and that they could head to the tents to wait for breakfast.

Most of the workers took another opportunity to cast surly glares at Dalton. Then they trooped off without a backwards glance, leaving him with Thomas.

They stood in silence until the men had disappeared from view. Then Thomas looked around.

Sounds of activity came from the chuck wagon, but nobody else other than the early detail were showing any signs of being awake. Thomas rubbed his hands with glee.

'Now we get to work,' he said, 'and we'll give everyone an awakening they'll never forget.'

Thomas directed Dalton to join him in heading to the edge. He scrambled down the slope into the gulch for a few paces and returned with a bundle that had been stashed away in the shadows.

He handed it to Dalton who unfolded the cloth to reveal six sticks of dynamite strapped together along with a short length of rope.

'That should wake everyone up,' Dalton said, turning the dynamite over in his hands.

'You want to keep watch or to plant it?'

'I'll plant it,' Dalton said, figuring that keeping hold of the sticks was the best way of ensuring they didn't get lit. He looked around for Seth and Caleb. 'What are the other two doing?'

'They're getting into position to cause more mayhem while the bridge is disappearing into the gulch.' Thomas chuckled. 'In fact, nobody's around so I reckon I'll join them.'

Thomas indicated the main stanchion and gave him quick instructions on how to plant it. Then, with a pat on the back, he turned to the tents leaving Dalton to make his way on to the bridge.

He walked slowly with the bundle held under his jacket while watching Thomas recede into the gloom. The sounds the stirring workers were making were now growing and so he figured he'd be able to get word to Victor before long.

That just left him with the problem of what to do with the dynamite and he figured that the simplest plan would be the best.

So he stopped at the stanchion Thomas had indicated. He knelt and acting stealthily, in case Thomas was watching him, he slipped the dynamite out of the bundle.

He reached over the side of the bridge and placed it on a plank two feet down.

He would need to check nobody was looking at him before tipping the dynamite over the side and letting it fall into the river below. Then he would apparently retire to a safe distance while instead he found Victor to warn him of the likely repercussions to come after the lack of an explosion.

While still presenting the image of a man carrying out his task, he placed the matches beside the dynamite. Then he unfurled the rope and lay down on his chest to reach down.

He stayed in this position while moving his arms for long enough to have tied the dynamite in place then moved to get up.

'What are you doing, Dalton?' a voice demanded behind him.

Dalton flinched. Then he looked up to find that Booth had sought him out.

'I was checking out the bridge while I waited for breakfast.'

'But that's not your job. What were you fiddling with down there?'

Booth moved to look over the side, but Dalton

took his arm and leaned forward to speak into his ear.

'Don't look down,' he whispered. 'Trust me on this. Your life is in danger, as is mine.'

'How can I trust you?' Booth asked. Despite his question, he lowered his voice.

'I don't blame you if you can't, but the horse bolting yesterday wasn't what it seemed. I'm secretly helping Victor to expose what Thomas, Seth and Caleb are doing.'

Booth jerked upright. He narrowed his eyes as he considered him in the growing morning light.

'I'm a good judge of character and the first time I saw you I thought you a decent man. Everything you've done since has tested that belief.' He flashed a smile. 'But you've been acting strangely and that's a more welcome explanation than the one I'd come up with.'

Dalton winked then beckoned for Booth to watch what he did next. He leaned over the side and struck a match, ensuring he was some distance from the dynamite. He let it flare and splutter for long enough to be seen by anyone paying close attention before shaking it out.

With a casual gesture he tipped the sticks of dynamite over the side. He watched them until they dropped out of sight into the gloom at the bottom of the gulch. When he heard a faint plop, he stood.

'After they'd blown up the bridge, Seth and the

others aimed to raise hell amongst the workers, so we need to find Victor and warn him.'

Booth nodded. He moved to go but then stopped.

'Where else were you supposed to plant dynamite?'

Booth's urgent tone made Dalton swing round to face him.

'Nowhere,' he said. 'What's on your mind?'

'Planting dynamite on the central stanchion would damage the bridge, but not enough to make it collapse.'

'What would?'

'I'm no expert.' Booth glanced around. 'But I'd place dynamite on the two end stanchions, and a lot of it.'

'Then perhaps their plan is only to issue Victor with a warning.'

The two men looked at each other, both noting with their winces that Seth and his men hadn't struck them as being the sort who acted in a half-hearted manner. Booth dropped to lie on the edge of the bridge.

He peered underneath along the length of the bridge then grunted. He bade Dalton to join him and pointed out what was worrying him.

At first Dalton could see nothing, but when his eyes became accustomed to the gloom beneath the bridge his gaze alighted on a glow.

At the end of the bridge a long burning fuse, that

presumably had been lit earlier, was fizzing down through the last inch towards the mass of dynamite strapped there.

'Run!' Dalton shouted, slapping Booth on the shoulder then pointing to the opposite end of the bridge.

'We can't go that way either,' Booth shouted. He pointed out another tied-up bunch of dynamite at the opposite end. 'They've planted dynamite on both sides.'

Dalton looked where Booth was pointing. Sparks were spluttering as another fuse burnt down through the last inch towards the dynamite.

'We're trapped in the middle,' he murmured, 'and this bridge is going to blow up at any second.'

CHAPTER 8

Dalton and Booth leapt to their feet and with no way of knowing if they'd live to get beyond the end of the bridge before it blew up, they chose the direction that took them towards the tents.

They pounded across the timbers. Dalton gritted his teeth as he got closer to the source of the imminent explosion while still having no choice but to run that way. They had halved the distance when a deafening roar went up behind them throwing them to the bridge on their chests.

He glanced at Booth to check he was fine and from his sprawled position to his side he returned a brief nod. Both men moved to get to their feet while hoping that the mismatch in the time between the two explosions would lengthen out for a few more precious seconds.

The bridge fell away, again knocking them on to their chests. Dalton fought to get upright, but the wood was tilting away in sudden jerking movements and knocking him down every time.

He looked over his shoulder to see that the explosion had ripped through the bridge. The main stanchion was tumbling away while the bulk of the bridge was collapsing.

Dalton scrambled for traction, but again the bridge jerked as the structure pivoted downwards towards the bottom of the gulch.

'We can't get off,' Booth screeched as he slipped backwards.

'We can't,' Dalton shouted. 'So just find something to hang on to.'

Dalton took his own advice and grabbed a plank that had been set sideways. He looked down to see that Booth had grabbed a plank running lengthways and had wrapped his arms around it. Then they both hung on, hoping that when the bridge fell, it would fall intact.

Another jerking movement lowered the bridge to a forty-five degree angle. Then it stopped moving. Dalton held his breath and gripped the wood firmly, expecting another collapse imminently. But long moments passed with the only change being the creaking and crashing as other parts the bridge toppled.

Hoping that the bridge had found a natural settled position, he looked to the opposite side of the gulch.

Rising dust blocked his view, but he could make out the outline of the bridge and the topmost section appeared to have settled on a lower tier. It was a precarious position, but for now it didn't look as if there'd be more movement.

He looked up to see that the shocked workers were peering over the side at the debris.

'Anyone down there?' Victor shouted from amongst the workers.

'Get back!' Dalton shouted. 'Both sides of the bridge have been dynamited.'

'And it could go off at any second,' Booth shouted.

Victor gave a curt nod. Then he moved out of sight shouting at others to stay away from the bridge while also delivering orders to find Seth, Thomas and Caleb. He could have saved his breath as gunfire then broke out from the direction of the tents as presumably Seth's group embarked on the second part of their plan to cause mayhem.

Dalton looked down to check that Booth was still below, then adopted his posture of wrapping his arms around a lengthways plank. He slid down it to reach Booth's side.

They briefly discussed the best way to get to safety and then side by side they slid down the angled bridge putting distance between themselves and the impending explosion. But despite expecting the dynamite to go off at any moment, they reached the next tier without mishap.

From this lower position Dalton could see the section of the encampment that was closest to the edge of the gulch. The shooting was petering out and Seth was being held from behind while Thomas and Caleb were escorted away. Other men were standing side-on to the bridge and peering about as they searched for the dynamite while shouting terse comments to each other.

Dalton and Booth continued to put distance between themselves and the possible explosion, and by the time they had worked themselves down to the bottom of the gulch, the workers reported that the dynamite had failed to explode. So Dalton and Booth headed to the pulley and climbed into a basket to be hauled to the top.

Despite the apparent good news, when they reached the top they wasted no time in getting out of the basket and hurrying away from the end of the bridge.

'Where do you think you're going?' Victor called after them, leading a group of men.

'When you've nearly been blown up,' Dalton said, turning to him, 'you don't want to risk it happening again.'

'I can see that.' Victor gestured to the men. Then he fixed Dalton with a stern glare that gave no hint that they had an agreement. 'So we'll keep you under guard until we uncover the truth about what happened here.'

In short order two men moved in and secured Booth while two more grabbed Dalton.

'You've got it wrong,' Dalton muttered as he was thrown into the cage after Booth, but like his previous pleas it was ignored.

He rolled to a halt then moved to leap out through the door, but a snort sounded behind him. He turned to find that Seth, Thomas and Caleb had already been imprisoned.

The group glared at him until Dalton went to sit beside Booth at the opposite side of cage. Booth considered him with a sorry shake of the head.

'I'm sorry,' Booth said, talking quietly so that the others couldn't hear.

'This isn't your fault,' Dalton said.

'It is. I told Victor you'd been acting suspiciously. He must have got it into his head that you were playing a dangerous game.'

'Don't worry.' Dalton noted that Seth was straining to hear their conversation so he spoke up. 'We've been tarred with the same brush as they have.'

Seth chuckled. 'It's worse than that for you. When Frank gets here he'll kill you.'

'Why?' Dalton asked.

'Frank Kelley has White Falls sown up. Nothing happens here without his agreement and anyone who crosses him gets a warning.' Seth laughed. 'They don't live to get a second warning.'

'But Frank was just someone Cliff Sinclair hired in Two Forks.'

Thomas and Seth looked at each other and shook their heads.

'That's the way Frank operates. He starts small, works his way in, and before long you're relying on him for protection, of a kind.'

Dalton nodded. 'And so you've decided Victor will never pay up?'

Seth nodded towards the gully indicating the remnants of the bridge.

'That was a warning,' he said. 'The next time we won't be so understanding.'

Dalton shook his head. 'Did Frank tell you to blow up the bridge?'

'He told us to make trouble.'

'Then you'll be the ones on the receiving end of the trouble. The likes of Frank threaten and push, but they don't destroy. All that'll happen now is the railroad will hire guns to get rid of you.'

Seth sneered, but he didn't reply immediately, proving that Dalton had been right. His group had been given a free hand to cause trouble, but it hadn't occurred to them that they might have gone too far.

'You've got no reason to gloat,' Seth snapped, regaining his former arrogant attitude. 'When Frank gets here, you'll get shot up long before he turns on us.'

The three men chuckled as the taunt made Dalton lower his head.

'Frank's coming,' Seth said, pointing at a commotion over by the tents.

'Then we'll be free soon,' Thomas said.

'And they'll die,' Caleb said.

The three men turned to look at Booth and Dalton and laughed. Then they returned to watching what was happening outside.

The day had passed slowly as the workers had inspected the damage. Although nobody had come close to the cage, the grumbling and slouched postures showed that nobody was happy.

So when a man opened the cage door and a gruff voice demanded that they get out, Dalton wasn't surprised that the workers gravitated towards the cage to present them with a mass of aggrieved glares.

With much angry muttering the workers grouped up, leaving only a thin passageway ahead to an open area beside the bridge. Seth, Thomas and Caleb went out first, but then they stopped, unwilling to be the first to run the gauntlet of the workers' ire.

So Dalton and Booth climbed out of the cage and headed down the aisle. Dalton was pleased that the workers only eyed them with suspicion, suggesting they felt that their role in the disaster had been misunderstood.

They emerged from the line unscathed to stand

before Victor. Behind them the others followed and this time the workers jeered and spat at them.

'Don't look pleased with yourselves,' Victor said. 'I'm not convinced yet that you had nothing to do with this.'

Victor pointed, drawing their attention to the bridge – or at least to what was left of it. Since they'd been imprisoned, it'd settled further down into the gulch with the top layer creating a large 'V' shape that rested on the bottom layer. To Dalton's untrained eye it was beyond salvage and would need rebuilding.

'We tried to stop that happening,' Dalton said.

Victor snorted. 'Either you didn't try hard enough, or you did just enough to look as if you were trying to stop it. But Frank Kelley will be here soon. I'll find out the truth then.'

'And you're going to let the man who's responsible for that mess calmly ride into here?'

Victor glanced over Dalton's shoulder making Dalton turn and see that Seth and the others were struggling to extricate themselves from the workers who were making the most of the opportunity to shove and shout abuse at them.

'Sure. He'll get to ride in calmly. But he won't get to leave.' Victor smirked. 'And you men are the bait.'

CHAPTER 9

The sun was descending beyond the far hills when Dalton caught his first sight of Frank Kelley.

He was confidently leading the riders who had tried to capture him two days ago, showing no concern that he might be riding into a trap.

Victor had situated his captives beside the bridge so that Frank would have to come into the centre of the camp to claim them. Although they hadn't been tied up or secured, several men were guarding them and their only escape route was the unpromising chasm of the gulch.

The workers had retreated to the tents where Dalton presumed that an ambush was being planned. What form it would take he didn't know.

Frank rode slowly on until he drew to a halt forty yards from the gathering, this being far enough away to beat a retreat but close enough to talk.

'You ready to talk business?' he hollered.

'It's too late for that,' Victor shouted back. 'There's nothing to protect now but a heap of broken wood.'

Frank raised himself in the saddle and when that failed to give him a clear view of the debris, he and the rest moved closer. The men halted ten yards on and glanced at each other in surprise before Frank smirked.

'You seem to have had some trouble there, but with my help you should get that mess cleared away quickly and get back on schedule.'

'And what kind of help would that be?'

Frank narrowed his eyes. 'The kind that avoids that happening again.'

Victor nodded as if he were mulling over the offer, giving Seth the opportunity to sidle closer to Dalton.

'Seems you got it wrong,' he said from the corner of his mouth. 'Frank's not concerned about what we did.'

With a mocking sideways movement Seth moved away from Dalton showing that he getting out of Frank's line of fire.

'He hasn't seen all the damage yet,' Dalton said, making Seth's confident grin waver.

Their conversation made Victor look at them before he cast a significant glance at a man to his left. That man slowly moved away to carry out whatever order he'd been given.

'I'm not paying you nothing, Frank,' Victor said.

'The only person paying anything is you for destroying my bridge.'

Frank glared at Victor, but even though he hadn't shown any sign of having noticed him Dalton found it impossible to keep quiet.

'And you'll pay for killing Loren Steele and Sheriff Blake,' he shouted, 'and for burning down my home.'

Frank turned to him, his eyes narrowing, showing that he hadn't spotted him before. He gestured to two men to seize him.

'We'll take this man off your hands,' he said.

'You won't,' Victor said. 'Now that I know the truth, you're doing nothing with him.'

Frank ignored him and with the other two men he moved on. He rode for ten yards, but then he came to a sudden halt as he got a full view of the gulch and the devastation there. He raised his eyebrows and tipped back his hat then shot a glare at Seth.

It was so piercing that Seth gulped. Then, with Thomas and Caleb, he shuffled backwards for an uncertain pace.

Victor caught the rising tension and behind his back he gestured. Hands strayed towards holsters.

Frank merely smiled, seemingly unconcerned that the eight men with Victor were preparing to draw their guns when only he and two other men were close enough to take them on. His other men stayed by the tents where they appeared more concerned about danger coming from that direction than from Victor's gunmen.

'Give me Dalton,' Frank said, leaning forward in the saddle. 'This is your only warning.'

Victor smiled, as if he'd been waiting for Frank to escalate the confrontation. Then, without comment, he raised a hand.

His gunmen drew their guns and levelled them on Frank, but still he didn't register concern. Casually he looked back at his men. In a mocking repetition of Victor's action, he raised a hand.

Victor tensed and moved for his own gun, but then he stilled the motion when every one of his gunmen swung their guns round to aim them at him.

'What are you doing?' he murmured, backing away for a pace.

'I'm making you pay the hard way,' Frank said with a shrug. 'You didn't think I'd entrust only those three idiots with keeping you in line, did you?'

Victor gave a resigned nod, looking as if he'd accept he'd been outmanoeuvred, but then he threw his hand to his gun.

He managed to draw the weapon before gunfire tore into him from several directions. As the bullets whined he writhed in a final dance of death before tumbling to the ground, repeatedly holed. Then Frank nodded towards Victor's former captives.

His final comment had confirmed Dalton's theory that he wasn't impressed to see the whole bridge destroyed. So before anyone could turn to them, Seth and Thomas turned on their heels and ran.

Dalton and Booth exchanged a brief glance then set off after them, but Caleb stayed, a smile on his lips as he moved towards Frank.

Dalton didn't see what happened next as he concentrated on putting distance between himself and the gunmen, but he heard the result as gunfire tore out followed by the sound of a body hitting the dirt.

All that was ahead was the edge of the gulch, but beside the bridge the ground didn't drop away as sharply as elsewhere so they should be able to find shelter.

Gunfire roared again, this time kicking dust at Dalton's heels. Reckoning that the gunmen would get him in their sights for the next volley, Dalton dived to the ground.

His momentum sent him sliding across the ground past Seth and Thomas until with a final scrambling roll he disappeared over the edge of the gulch. His hope that he would find shelter proved founded when he landed on a ledge three feet down from the top.

As another volley tore out, the other three men dived into cover beside him. Then they scrambled round to sit with their backs to the rock where despite their previous enmity they looked at each and smiled at their good fortune.

More shots rang out, but this time they were

further away. Dalton risked looking over the edge to see that Frank had turned away from them, clearly judging that they wouldn't cause him trouble, and had turned his attention on to the tents.

The men he'd situated near to the tents were moving in on the workers and these men were scurrying into hiding while others were taking up defensive positions to fight them off.

Dalton shot a glance at his companions, requesting suggestions on what they could do to help them. Thomas and Seth were sitting hunched, probably in shock at having Frank turn on them. Booth though had joined Dalton in looking over the edge.

'I hate to say this,' he said, 'but we can't do nothing. We need to get into hiding under the bridge.'

'You can hide,' Dalton said, shaking his head. 'I'm doing something.'

Despite his comment, if he were to come out of hiding he couldn't see anything he could do other than to die. Then his gaze alighted on Victor's body and his six-shooter, lying twenty paces away. Dalton smiled then waited for the right moment to make a run for it.

The gunmen were joining the rest of Frank's men and none of them were looking at the gulch. So he rolled over on to the level ground.

When nobody reacted he adopted a shuffling gait and bent double he edged towards Victor. He kept his weight balanced on both feet so that if anyone were to see him he could run to safety, but after ten paces he reached the point where it would be quicker to go for the gun.

He speeded up, but in doing so his foot slid on a stone and he went to one knee.

One of the gunmen flinched then looked his way. He took in the sight of Dalton without concern, but then he saw where he had been heading. He crouched, his gun swinging round to aim at him.

Dalton didn't wait for him to get a bead on him and he ran for Victor's body. He covered three paces quickly then threw himself to the ground, the action saving him from a bullet that whined over his back.

On his belly he skidded into Victor's side then gathered up the gun. Another shot tore into Victor's prone body, but by then Dalton had managed to swing the gun up and with it propped on Victor's side he took aim.

A single shot dispatched the gunman, sending him tumbling backwards on to his back.

Dalton then turned his attention on to the other gunmen.

These men were still moving away from him, so he took the opportunity to unhitch Victor's gunbelt. Then, judging that the body was providing inade-quate cover, he looked around for the nearest place from which to launch an assault.

The best available cover was a pile of lumber that

had been removed from the destroyed bridge. He jumped to his feet, but before he could move towards it, two gunmen looked back and saw their fallen associate.

They both uttered a cry of warning and as one the rest of the gunmen turned. A solid line of guns turned on him.

Dalton didn't reckon he could take on all the gunslingers and neither did he think he could reach the lumber pile. So he turned on his heels.

On the run he splayed two wild shots over his shoulder and several returned shots kicked dirt beside his feet before he scrambled over the edge to find that Booth and the rest were no longer there.

He looked around, the motion putting him back into the gunmen's view. A shot winged past his ear. He ducked down and this time he saw Booth gesturing at him from within the bridge debris. He returned a grateful nod then crawled along the ledge to join him.

Seth and Thomas were also hiding beneath the sloping timbers that this morning had been the top of the bridge. There, the shadows and the mass of wood above them provided cover, but when four gunmen appeared on the edge of the gulch they took only a few seconds to turn their gazes towards the bridge.

One man pointed while another aimed his gun at them, but before he could fire Dalton blasted lead at them. His shots were wild, but they made the men jerk out of view.

As gunfire continued to rip out from the direction of the tents showing that the workers were fighting for their lives, only two men stayed to exchange gunfire with them. Every few moments they bobbed up and took pot shots. Each time Dalton returned gunfire.

Neither side hit a target, but the stand-off was unlikely to continue for much longer without someone being hit. Booth tapped Dalton's shoulder.

'We need to get further away while we still can,' he said.

'We stay.' Dalton paused to listen to the gunfire peeling out. 'The workers need our help.'

Booth didn't reply while he listened to the gunfire exchanges.

'One armed man won't be able to help them, and there's a chance this won't turn out well. Then Frank's gunmen will come for us.'

A man slipped into view and blasted off a shot. This time the lead tore splinters from the wood above Dalton's head and then ricocheted beneath the bridge kicking more splinters from the heap of wood Seth was hiding behind.

Seth winced then jumped up to offer support.

'I agree,' he said. 'We put distance between us and the gunmen.'

Although Dalton hated the thought of agreeing

with a man who until a few minutes ago had worked for Frank Kelley, he provided a reluctant nod then gestured for Booth to choose the route.

Booth didn't need a second request and he pointed out where they needed to go beneath the fallen top layer to get down into the gulch. Then he set off. Seth and Thomas fell in behind him leaving Dalton to guard the rear.

Booth found a twisting route between the fallen timbers that had enough wood on either side to keep them protected. After covering twenty yards raised voices went up behind proving that their retreat had been noticed and that they were being followed, but Dalton also heard curses so he reckoned that their pursuers hadn't found such a good route.

All the time gunfire raged, but the sounds got further away.

'What you reckon is happening back there, Seth?' Dalton called ahead.

'Frank is shooting up the workers,' Seth said.

'Was that the plan all along?'

Seth stopped to look at Dalton. 'No. He was trying to muscle in on the railroad operations. But he must have decided to cut his losses.'

Dalton winced. Nobody spoke again until Booth slipped between two fallen planks and came out on the top of the bridge. When Dalton joined him, he saw that they were at the lowest point of the collapsed structure.

From here, they could pick a route down to the bottom of the gulch, but then they'd be in the open where they could be picked off easily from the top of the gulch, so Booth pointed upwards.

'Plenty of horses got stranded on the other side,' he said. 'If we can get up there, we can get away.'

Dalton looked along the route he'd indicated. With the far side of the bridge being the half that had been dynamited, the structure ahead was more damaged than the section they'd traversed. There didn't appear to be any routes up other than to do as Booth suggested and clamber over the wood.

He slapped Booth on the back. 'Then do it, but do it quickly.'

Booth agreed with this sentiment and so they made their hurried way over the centre of the bridge and then followed him up the other side. They walked for only a dozen yards before the slope became too steep for them to walk. Then they had to clamber on hands on knees to gain height and after another dozen yards they had to climb as if the mass of wood was a rock face.

Every few seconds Dalton looked back to check on whether their pursuers had come into view, but they didn't appear, presumably as they struggled to find a way out of the fallen bridge.

The final stretch was sheer, leading to a mass of fallen wood on the edge of the gulch. Booth again took the lead and he clambered up with a mixture of sure-footed confidence and urgency.

Seth and then Thomas followed on behind at his heels while Dalton stood guard until they'd gained some height. Then, as he needed two hands, he holstered his gun and climbed.

He followed the route Thomas was taking, grabbing hold of the lengths of fallen timbers until he was directly below him. Every time Thomas lifted his foot Dalton slapped his hand down and drew himself up. They had to climb for around sixty feet and Dalton had covered half the distance when Booth rolled out of view.

Seth had clambered up to a point below the edge when Booth crept back into sight. He thrust a hand down to Seth while beckoning for Thomas and Dalton to hurry.

'The bridge is solid up here,' he said. 'We can reach firm ground.'

Seth grunted that he understood as he let Booth pull him up. Then both men reached down to help Thomas. Booth grabbed an arm while Seth slapped a hand on his back and they worked together to roll him over the side.

A gunshot tore out, spraying splinters and forcing the three men to flinch away out of Dalton's sight. Dalton was six feet from the top. He resisted the urge to look down to see where the shot had come from. But when another volley tore into the wood beside his head, he looked back.

The two pursuers had now emerged from the tangle of broken wood. One man was clambering over the bottom of the bridge while the other man had found a good vantage point. He was hidden well so that Dalton would find it hard to hit him, but with his hands resting on a fallen beam for stability he was aiming up at him with assurance.

The man fired, and the shot winged into the wood a foot to Dalton's side. The man then reloaded, but with him having got Dalton in his sights it would be only a matter of a few more shots before he got lucky.

Dalton reached up and drew himself up another foot as Seth and Thomas appeared above.

'Throw me your gun,' Seth said. 'I'll give him something to worry about.'

Dalton shook his head and continued to climb. A shot clattered into the wood inches from his fingers making him jerk the hand back. The movement almost unbalanced him and he wheeled his free arm until he righted himself then hugged the bridge.

'Do it,' Booth said, appearing above him. 'No matter how little we trust these men, we're all in the same mess now.'

As Seth cast Booth an aggrieved glare, Dalton shook his head, but another slug tore into the bridge beside his raised arm, and this time it was close enough to fray cloth.

With a resigned sigh, he gripped a plank with his left hand, then reached down to his holster. He hefted the six-shooter on his palm then launched the weapon up towards Seth, but he'd never tried to throw while clinging hold of a sheer wall before and he misjudged the strength needed.

The weapon turned end over end as it rose limply. Then it clattered into the timber wall two feet below the edge. Seth lunged for it and tipped the barrel with a finger, but he couldn't get a firm grip and the weapon fell away.

Dalton thrust out a hopeful hand, but the gun fell several feet to his left and he could do nothing but watch it fall away. Then, with a hollow feeling in his guts, he raised his gaze to the shooter.

That man had his gun trained on him, his shoulders hunched with confidence. The other man had now reached the bottom of the wall directly below him. And he had turned his gun on him too.

CHAPTER 10

'You dropped our only gun,' Dalton shouted, more in anger at himself than at Seth.

Seth gave him a narrowed-eyed glare and it was left to Booth to state the obvious.

'Stop standing around and get up here before they shoot you.'

Dalton took one last look at the gunmen below then took the advice. He gritted his teeth and concentrated on his climbing.

He threw up a hand, grabbed a higher hold and dragged himself up. Then he repeated the motion.

More shots sounded below but he was concentrating so well that he didn't note where they landed.

A firm tug on his right wrist made him flinch, thinking that he'd been hit. Then he saw Booth's hand around his wrist. He locked hands with him and when he moved his other hand to a higher position Seth grabbed it.

97

Together the two men drew him up.

A final volley tore out and ripped along the wood, hammering lead to either side of Dalton's dangling legs. Then they dragged him over the top and out of sight.

The four men lay on the top of the pile of wood gathering their breath while Dalton looked to the edge of the gulch.

The dynamite had destroyed the end of the bridge, but the broken planks had fallen in a position that provided a precarious passage to solid ground.

Dalton was about to congratulate Booth, but he and the other two were staring agog across the gulch. Dalton followed their gazes and what he saw there made him wince.

The tents were ablaze and most of Frank Kelley's men were standing in a line. The gunfire had stopped, and although from their position close to the top of the gulch he couldn't see what they were doing, it was clear the battle was over.

Some workers were fleeing, but several of Frank's men were dragging bodies aside.

Then, as if he'd detected their interest, Frank Kelley looked across the gulch and from seventy-five yards away he and Dalton locked gazes.

Frank sneered then gestured for the men who were not involved in dealing with the bodies to head on to the bridge.

'Time to go,' Dalton said.

Booth nodded and set off, but Thomas risked a glance over the edge at the gunmen below then shook his head.

'We won't get far,' he said. 'Those men are at our heels.'

'Then we need to stop them,' Seth said.

Thomas grunted that he agreed and after a brief muttered conversation with Seth, the two men located an unattached ten-foot long plank. They dragged it to the edge and tipped it over the side.

Before it'd clattered down to the base of the bridge they'd located a second plank and pushed it over. This time they got the response they wanted when a cry of pain tore out.

Dalton looked over the edge to see that the gunman who had been climbing had been knocked down to the bottom of the bridge. He was now lying on his back beneath the plank.

The second man had stayed out of range of the falling debris and on seeing them he tore off a shot that made them all jerk back and out of view.

'We've got plenty of planks to throw down,' Thomas said, smiling at their success. 'We can bruise plenty of heads.'

'You can, but I'd prefer to put some distance between Frank and us.'

Dalton shuffled back from the edge and appraised the mess of wood at the top of the bridge. Then he called Booth over and outlined his idea.

Booth smiled and, with a rub of his hands, he cast an expert eye over the mess of broken wood.

After kicking several planks, he located a beam that was vital for holding up the remnants of the bridge. Then, while Seth and Thomas enjoyed themselves tipping planks over the side, Dalton and Thomas put their hands to the beam.

Their first attempt to move it didn't shift it even an inch and even when they flexed their backs and strained the beam remained still. So Booth located a shorter plank that lay beneath the beam that was sticking up almost vertically and they dragged down on that instead.

With the plank acting as a lever, the beam rose up a foot from the strut that was below it and then slowly swung round. Timbers ground as the movement put extra strain on the already precarious structure.

Seth and Thomas stopped throwing planks over the edge to watch them. When they saw what they were doing, they pushed one last plank over the side. Then they joined them in pulling down on the end of the plank.

Their help made the plank creak and Dalton thought that they were likely to break it before anything else gave way. But other planks and pieces of debris started to fall away and slip over the edge, lessening the weight on the main beam.

As the slow trickle of wood became a torrent, the

beam itself speeded its movement. Inexorably the four men dragged the plank lower and the beam continued to rise.

With the strain on the whole structure becoming critical the beam shook, almost dislodging them. Booth gestured with his head pointing out the route to solid ground.

'The moment you feel it go, we release the beam,' he said. 'Then we run for our lives.'

Grunted acknowledgements came from the other three as they continued to strain. They dragged the plank down to waist level and then down to their knees, making the beam open up a clear gap as it parted from the strut below it.

'Just another foot,' Dalton muttered, the words emerging as gasps as he strained.

The beam swung away from the strut below, but then another movement caught his eye.

A hand, then an arm appeared over the top of the wooden wall they'd climbed earlier. Then the first of their pursuers got both his arms on the top and dragged himself up.

'Run,' Thomas shouted. He released the beam and ran for safety.

Taken by surprise the other three men held on, but the strain of holding up the beam was too great and with no choice they all looked at each other and nodded. With a co-ordinated move, they released the plank.

The beam they'd raised thudded down, bounced, flexed and then rolled towards the man who'd just reached the top.

The man glanced around looking for an escape route, but he was too slow. The beam hit him squarely in the chest and he and the beam went flying over the side.

The wood that had been lying on the beam was catapulted into the air. The strut that had been below the beam creaked and bowed out, spraying splinters, but none of the men waited to see what happened next.

Heedless of the safest route they scrambled and leapt over the broken planks, trusting that their speed and desperation would find them a safe passage.

A cry went up behind him, but Dalton ignored it and with a diving leap, he threw himself over the last lengths of wood and slammed his chest to the solid earth. He lay enjoying the feel of the ground then turned to see that the others had reached the side.

He looked to the bridge and it was to see that Booth had picked the right beam to remove to topple the structure. The bridge was doomed. With a thunderous series of cracks, the structure fell away carrying tons of wood and their pursuers with it.

The sight was so awe-inspiring that they didn't think of making their escape as they watched the bridge that so many men had worked to put up fall into the gulch it was supposed to span.

When the debris settled the first section of the bridge on the other side of the gulch remained standing, but between the point where they'd started climbing to the edge of the gulch there was a gaping chasm.

Best of all Dalton judged that it was a chasm Frank Kelley wouldn't be able to ford.

That thought made him look up and through the rising dust he picked out Frank on the other side. He was standing with his legs planted wide apart also staring at the fallen bridge. But perhaps sensing that Dalton was looking at him, he looked up.

He tipped his hat to him with a mocking gesture then pointed a firm finger at him that said this matter didn't end there.

Dalton returned a gesture of his own and murmured a silent promise that he would make him pay for what he'd done to Loren. Then he turned away, not waiting to see what he did next, and joined his new companions.

'Find the horses,' he said to Booth. 'Then we ride.'

'How long do you reckon we've got?' Seth asked.

'It'll take Frank a while to get across the gulch,' Dalton said, 'but there's a crossing point about ten miles downriver.'

Booth sighed. 'And then he'll be a-coming for us.'

The others murmured that they agreed with this

gloomy forecast after which silence reigned.

They'd ridden into the night towards White Falls seeking to put as much distance as they could between themselves and the bridge. As they were worried about the reception Seth and Thomas would get there, they'd camped a few miles out of town at a high point where they could look down on the town.

It was a measure of the bond the mismatched group had forged in a short time that they hadn't argued about stopping here even though Dalton and Booth had nothing to fear. But Seth's comment brought home to Dalton that they needed to discuss this issue.

'We need a plan,' he said. 'We've got no weapons and no allies. We need to find both.'

'Where?' Seth said, with a significant glance at the few lights visible in White Falls.

'We both know where, so I reckon it's time for you to tell us why you're worried about going into town.'

Seth rubbed his chin as he considered, then shrugged.

'I guess I've got no reason. I've never been there, and either way I doubt anyone would be concerned about what we did at the bridge after what Frank did.'

With Seth acquiescing everyone looked at Thomas.

'I don't want to talk to no lawman,' he said. He looked around into the darkness and shivered. 'But I don't like sitting out here waiting to be found either.'

Dalton nodded then stood. 'In that case I know somewhere safer where you can hole up while I find Deputy Lawton.'

This offer cheered everyone and so they stamped out their fire and headed off to find the place where Wes Potter had said he was staying, a small house a few miles beyond the opposite side of town.

The stars told Dalton that it was approaching midnight when in the sallow light from the rising moon he caught his first sight of the house. There was a corral, but no horses, making Thomas grumble.

'It's deserted,' he said.

'Then that's fine,' Dalton said. 'I can leave you here while I head into town.'

Thomas still muttered unhappily while casting concerned looks over his shoulder as if Frank was about to pounce on him at any moment. They dismounted at the corral.

Booth and Seth stayed outside to check for signs of anyone having followed them while Thomas and Dalton hurried to the door. Dalton signified that Thomas should stand back in case Wes was here, after all.

He knocked on the door. When that motion made the door rattle, he called out. He didn't get a response and so he pushed the door, but the door tipped away and went crashing down with a loud thud.

'Anything wrong?' Booth asked from the shadows.

'I don't know,' Dalton said. He shivered despite the warm evening then paced on to the fallen door and inside.

Thomas followed him in and looked around until Dalton waved at him to stop blocking the light. He moved away from the door, but that only made Dalton wish he hadn't.

The moonlight streaming in through the door illuminated a pool of liquid that glistened darkly beside a table. Dalton moved around the table while peering into the darkness.

He discerned a shape on the floor. More liquid had spread around it.

As he approached, a rank smell invaded his nostrils, one he'd come across before when a dead animal was close by in the undergrowth. He looked up at Thomas, who was gulping and pointing at something he could see in the darkness on the other side of the door.

Now with an intense sense of foreboding Dalton gestured at him to investigate while he knelt beside the shape. He reached out and touched skin. When he drew the body into the moonlight it wasn't Wes's, but it was one of the former citizens of Two Forks, Chester Clarke.

Dalton looked up to see that Thomas had found a body too. Again this one wasn't Wes's, but again it was someone from Two Forks.

Dalton called out for the others to join him and Booth located a lamp. The harsh light flooded the room and outlined the bodies, making all the men wince.

They searched the house and after going through the two other rooms, Dalton found Wes, although he located two other bodies beforehand.

The five people who had died here had all been people from Two Forks. These men had taken Cliff Sinclair's money, but none of them had lived for long enough to benefit from it.

Although it was unclear what the sequence of events had been, Dalton reckoned it was a reasonable guess that after Cliff had paid these people, someone had followed them to claim back the money then killed them.

What he didn't know was whether Cliff had known this would happen. With Frank's involvement in events in the area being more insidious than he had thought, Dalton now wondered if Cliff had been as much a victim of Frank's murderous nature as these people had been. Certainly it would have been easier for him to have just disposed of the Two Forks folk back at the settlement rather than use such underhand methods.

'So,' Thomas said when they'd drawn the bodies into the main room, 'this place's not a safe haven, after all.'

'Nowhere is safe,' Booth murmured unhappily, 'any more.'

'Frank Kelley seems to be everywhere,' Dalton said, 'but that doesn't mean he's sown up the whole county. We just need to find a way to fight back.'

'One that these men didn't try?' Booth asked. 'There were more of them than there are of us, and they were probably armed, and—'

'Enough,' Seth snapped. 'If you're thinking like that, you might as well curl up and die. I'm with Dalton. We fight back.'

He gave one last stern look around the room. Then, with a determined tread, he headed to the door. He didn't look back to check the others would follow his lead as he stomped outside, but he'd managed only a single pace before he jerked back into the room and pressed his back to the wall.

His shocked expression told everyone what he'd seen outside. They'd been followed.

CHAPTER 11

'How many are out there?' Dalton asked.

Seth shrugged. 'I didn't stand around looking, but I only saw the one rider.'

'Then all's not lost yet.'

'It depends who the rider is,' Booth grumbled.

As Thomas added his own grumble Dalton went to the window and peered out between the shutters.

Seth and Thomas rooted around for something they could use to defend themselves. Booth took the other window and smiled the same as Dalton did.

'It is just the one man,' he called to Seth and Thomas, 'and he's saved Dalton from making a journey.'

'What do you mean?' Thomas snapped, brandishing a log he'd claimed from beside the fire.

Neither man got the time to answer before Deputy Lawton rode into view through the open doorway. He considered the fallen door then looked around while backing his horse away, but before he could get too worried Dalton walked into his line of sight and hailed him.

'I didn't know you'd come here as well,' Lawton said, 'but I was told Wes Potter wanted to see me.'

'He did,' Dalton said, 'but I can tell you now.'

Dalton gestured into the house. With a last cautious glance around, Lawton dismounted then headed inside. The sight that confronted him made him cast suspicious glances at the other three men and back away to the doorway, his hand drifting to his holster.

Booth smiled while Seth lowered his head. Thomas passed the log from hand to hand while glaring at the deputy.

'Are these Two Forks folk?' Lawton said, pointing at the bodies.

'Yeah,' Dalton said.

'And they'd all be people you disagreed with about talking Cliff Sinclair's money?'

'They are,' Dalton said, raising his hands and offering a placating smile, 'but I didn't have nothing to do with this. I might not have agreed with them about Cliff, but Wes was a good friend as were these people.'

'I wasn't suggesting anything.' Lawton took a pace into the house. 'But I'm interested in why you took that line.'

Dalton lowered his head while he thought out the

best way to convince the deputy of their innocence.

'I've got a long story to tell,' he said with a confident tone. 'I was coming to town to tell you about it, but it seems the situation is even worse than I thought.'

Dalton signified that Lawton should sit, but he ignored him.

'Does Sheriff Blake fit into the story?'

Dalton winced and took a few moments before he replied.

'It does,' he said, lowering his voice.

Lawton must have picked up Dalton's change of tone as this time he sat at the table. Dalton sat on the other side while the others moved in to join him.

Seth sat at one end while Booth sat at the other. Lawton nodded to each man and in turn they offered their names.

Thomas was the last to join them. With only one place to take he moved to sit beside Lawton, but as he passed behind the deputy he raised the log. He jerked forwards and with a backhanded swipe he swung the log at Lawton's head.

Dalton jumped to his feet with a warning cry on his lips, but he was already too late.

The log caught Lawton a stinging blow behind the right ear and knocked him forward. His head collided with the edge of the table and without a sound Lawton slipped down to the floor.

'Why?' Seth demanded, scraping back his chair.

Thomas rounded on him, but he kept the log held back ready to hit Lawton again if he stirred.

'You know we can't sit down with no lawman.'

'I don't. I've not done nothing that'd worry him.' Seth narrowed his eyes as he considered Thomas's sweating brow. 'But you have.'

Thomas conceded that point with a shrug. 'That don't change the fact we need to get away from here fast.'

'We do now,' Dalton said, 'but we didn't before you hit him. Lawton was all set to hear us out, but when he comes to he won't believe anything we tell him.'

'*If* he comes to.'

'Hey,' Booth said, standing. 'We're not making this situation any worse than it already is.'

Thomas darted his gaze from one man to the next. Dalton moved towards him, while Seth raised his hands in a calming gesture while shaking his head.

Thomas raised the log. 'The first man to take another step gets the same treatment as Lawton got.'

Seth caught Dalton's eye with a look that said they should co-ordinate their assault, but that encouraged Thomas to back away for a pace then drop to his knees.

Seth and Dalton moved around the table, but then they slid to a halt when they saw that Thomas had claimed the deputy's gun. He looked up at them from the floor, grinning.

'I'm the one giving the orders now,' he said.

'What you hoping to gain here?' Dalton demanded, although he did back away while raising his hands.

'I'm fighting back; that's what I'm doing. I've had enough of running, so if Frank Kelley finds me now, he'll regret it.'

'We should fight back,' Dalton said, speaking slowly. 'But we can't take him on. We need allies, and the law was the best option.'

'Not for me it wasn't. I'll take my chances.' He glanced at Seth. 'You ready to start taking my orders?'

'Nope,' Seth said, shaking his head. 'You're too much trouble.'

Thomas scowled. Then, with the gun thrust out, he backed away to the door. Nobody moved, giving him confidence that he wouldn't be waylaid and he speeded up then side-stepped through the door. A few moments later hoofbeats confirmed that he had abandoned them.

Dalton knelt beside the deputy. He was breathing smoothly.

'You made the right decision,' he said, looking at the others. 'But we have another one to make. Either we wait for the deputy to wake up and we explain ourselves, or we find somewhere else to hide.'

'We go,' Seth said. 'Lawton won't listen to our

excuses. And besides I'm getting a bad feeling about this place.'

Booth had been shaking his head, but the last comment made him glance at the bodies and shiver.

'I agree. We need to get away.'

Dalton's vote was that they should stay, but with him being outvoted and with Seth showing to his surprise that he was prepared to stay with them rather than go with Thomas, he nodded.

'All right,' he said. 'We go.'

'But where?' Booth asked as they headed to the door.

Dalton came to a halt as he considered.

'Thomas was right about one thing. We need to stop running and make a stand against Frank Kelley.' Dalton smiled for the first time in a while. 'And there's only one place where we can do that.'

'Cliff Sinclair won't be pleased to see you,' Booth said when the ranch house first came into view. 'You were the only one who was prepared to stand against him.'

'I've spent the last few weeks opposing him,' Dalton said, 'but I wonder now if I misunderstood him. I hope I got it wrong and he's just a decent man who Frank lied to and that once he knows what's happened to the homesteaders, he'll join with us against him.'

'That's a big leap of faith,' Seth said, while Booth

muttered that he agreed, although neither man offered an alternate option.

Two nights ago they had left the deputy in Wes Potter's house then rested up a few miles out of White Falls. At first light they'd headed south towards Two Forks. Constantly they'd looked over their shoulders expecting that either Frank Kelley or Deputy Lawton would have followed them, but late on the second day of travel they had reached the ranch gates unopposed.

Worryingly there was no sign of anyone near the normally bustling ranch house. The only sounds were the wind whistling nearby and the creaking of Cliff's water tower.

The men glanced at each other, conveying their thoughts on how the last time they'd approached a quiet house it'd turned out badly.

They dismounted at the corral. The last time Dalton had visited around twenty horses had been there. Now the fence had broken down and it was empty.

The three men turned on the spot looking for signs of life, or the opposite, but there was nothing.

'Do we split up and search on our own?' Booth asked with a shaking tone that suggested he was hoping for a negative answer.

'We stick together,' Dalton said. 'I've never known this place to be anything less than teeming with people.'

So after tethering their horses they headed to the house. They were twenty yards from the porch when a rifle shot rang out. They all flinched and looked around, but Dalton couldn't see anybody.

A second shot thundered, kicking dust five yards to their right. This time the sound and sighting of the shot let Dalton pinpoint the general direction of the shooter.

He turned from the house and looked at the barn. He saw no sign of anyone there. Then he looked past the well to the dry gulch that meandered by the water tower then to the water tower itself.

A stray flash of light from gunmetal drew his attention to the rifle held low on the edge of the tower.

Someone was standing inside the tower, presumably on a raised platform. This man acknowledged he'd be seen by calling out to them.

'You'll come no closer,' he shouted. 'Those were warning shots. The rest won't be.'

'Cliff Sinclair?' Dalton shouted.

'Yeah, and I can see it's you, Dalton. You're not welcome here, so ride off while you still can.'

The change in Cliff's voice surprised Dalton. It didn't have his usual authoritative tone and it had emerged as a strangulated screech.

Dalton murmured a quick command to the others to stay put. Then he raised his hands and walked slowly towards the tower.

Cliff had built the tower to resolve his water problems. It was an inverted dome, the iron now rusting. It had been set twenty feet off the ground on stilts and was thirty feet high. When full this impressive structure held thousands of gallons of water.

'We don't have to argue,' he said. 'I didn't accept your money, but that doesn't mean you have to run me off your land.'

Cliff raised himself into full view, but he still kept the rifle on him.

'I sure will. One day I will make this ranch work the way I want it to, and you and the rest won't stop me.'

Dalton nodded as Cliff confirmed that his anger wasn't solely directed at him.

'If I were to say I'll take your money, would that change your mind?'

Cliff lowered his head for a moment and softened his tone.

'I'm sorry about what happened to your house. It had nothing to do with me. Right now though I've got more on my mind than just your land.' Cliff shrugged. 'But maybe later we can talk terms.'

'I'm sorry that I can't do that,' Dalton said matching Cliff's conciliatory tone with a low tone of his own. 'Anybody who takes your money doesn't get to enjoy it.'

Cliff glared down at him, but when Dalton said nothing more he slapped the rim in frustration then lowered his rifle. He clambered out of the tower on to a ladder and climbed down.

'How many?' he asked when he joined him.

'I still hope that some got away, but the situation looks bad. We went to White Falls to hole up with Wes Potter. He was dead as were several others.'

Cliff gulped. 'I didn't know about that.'

Dalton searched Cliff's eyes, seeing the pain.

'I believe you.'

Cliff breathed a sigh of relief. He looked over Dalton's shoulder.

'Who are your friends?'

Before Dalton could reply Seth stepped forward.

'We're others,' he said, 'who oppose Frank Kelley.'

'It's a pity there's not more of you,' Cliff said, gesturing for them to join him in heading to the house, 'or we might have stood a chance when he comes.'

'You know for sure he'll return?' Dalton asked.

Cliff stopped and fixed Dalton with his tired gaze.

'If there's one thing I know about Frank, it's that he doesn't leave any loose ends.'

'Then,' Dalton said, 'we'll make him regret being careful.'

CHAPTER 12

'That's how Frank operates,' Seth said when they'd rested up in the house and listened to Cliff's tale of how Frank had wormed his way into his confidence. 'He arrives quietly, makes himself invaluable, but all the time he's working to undermine you.'

'I know,' Cliff said unhappily. 'I wanted to be fair to the Two Forks folk, but I thought there might be trouble, so I hired Frank. I had no idea what he was really doing until it was too late. Even ranch hands I'd employed recently turned out to be working for him.'

'And now there's just you left?'

'Just me.' Cliff went to the window and looked outside. 'But I built this place up from nothing. I can do it again.'

'But only,' Dalton said, 'after we've dealt with Frank.'

Cliff nodded. 'Is there any hope of more help coming?'

Dalton winced and glanced at Booth and Seth.

'Maybe not,' Booth said. 'Deputy Lawton knows about the trouble, and the railroad will know about what happened at the bridge, but unless someone's followed us here, I doubt anyone will help us.'

Cliff gave Booth an odd look then dismissed the matter with a shrug.

'Then we'll have to defend ourselves on our own.'

With that comment Cliff beckoned for them to follow him. He led them to his armoury, which when he unlocked the door presented enough firepower to cheer everyone for the first time since they'd formed their group.

By the time the sun was edging towards the distant mountains, they had organized themselves to withstand the likely onslaught. Cliff headed outside to resume his vigil in the water tower while Booth took up a position on the other side of the ranch to cover anyone approaching from the direction of the river.

Seth and Dalton stayed in the house and tried to sleep, but despite the limited rest they'd had last night neither man found it easy. They didn't talk much either.

Dalton found it odd that after he'd tried to kill him, Seth had become an ally. Despite Seth's apparent decision to turn his back on his past, Dalton still felt uneasy.

Finally he fell into a fitful sleep that had failed to rest him when Cliff woke him to take over the duty of keeping watch from the water tower. Cliff went outside with him and showed him the safe way to climb the tower.

When Dalton had clambered inside it was as he'd imagined it. The tower had a central bowl that was three-quarters full of water that shimmered in the moonlight, and there was a walkway that circled the tower set a few feet down on which he could sit.

From there he surveyed the terrain while waiting for the men he felt sure would come, but his watch passed quietly as did his final stretch before dawn.

For the new day, they needed only one man on duty as the tower provided a panoramic view. Cliff was eager to take that duty and so that left the others to wile away the day sitting on the porch and waiting.

They didn't have to wait for long.

The sun was halfway to its highest point when Cliff caught their attention with a wave. They moved away from the house to see that a rider was galloping closer while repeatedly looking over his shoulder.

'Help?' Booth asked hopefully.

'I don't think so,' Seth said, narrowing his eyes before he grunted with irritation. 'That's Thomas.'

'And at the speed he's pushing his horse,' Dalton said, 'I reckon he's fleeing for his life.'

As if to prove Dalton's assessment was right,

Thomas swerved in through the gates then drew up his horse with a sharp tug that made it rear. He jumped down before the sweat-licked mount had been able to stop then stomped to a halt.

He looked at them, his haggard expression obvious even from fifty yards away. Then he fell to his knees and keeled over on to his chest.

Despite everyone's antipathy after he'd abandoned them, the three men broke into a run and with Cliff covering them from the tower they hurried to Thomas's side. Thomas stayed on his chest and Dalton could see why. A red stain marred his lower back. When Booth placed a hand on his shoulder, he grunted at him to stay away.

'With that wound,' Booth said, 'I can't see what kept him going.'

'I wanted,' Thomas murmured, 'to die where Frank couldn't see me.'

'And that means he'll have followed you here,' Seth snapped.

Thomas raised himself and fixed Seth with a firm glare.

'He was coming anyhow. Frank ambushed me. I got away, but I reckoned I owed you a warning.'

'Obliged.' Seth patted his gun. 'But we're ready to face him.'

'I didn't mean Frank.' Thomas slapped his hands to the ground and strained to raise himself higher.

Dalton waited for an explanation of what he'd

meant, but Thomas flopped down and lay breathing shallowly.

'Get him some water,' Dalton said, gesturing to Booth.

'It's too late for him,' Seth said, pointing, 'and it's too late for us.'

Dalton followed his gaze to the water tower to see that Cliff was gesticulating beyond the ranch gates. He looked that way then winced.

Thomas had been followed.

At a more sedate pace than Thomas had used a line of riders was approaching. They were still a quarter mile away, but Dalton could discern that there were at least a dozen men.

They were heavily outnumbered, and those odds worsened when Thomas uttered a strangulated gasp then twitched and lay still. Booth moved to see if he could help him, but Dalton shook his head.

'Leave him,' Dalton said. 'We go to the house and make our stand.'

The others grunted that they agreed. Then, without further discussion, they hurried to the ranch house. The main room in which they settled had windows that faced in both directions, which ensured they couldn't be outflanked, but with there being only three of them this spread their defence thinly.

Dalton and Seth took up positions at the two front windows and Booth took the rear window. From there they watched Frank Kelley and his men make their steady way towards them through the gates.

Cliff had dropped down so the riders wouldn't be able to see him thus providing them with one surprise advantage.

'What do you reckon Thomas was trying to warn us about?' Seth asked.

'I hope,' Dalton said, 'it had something to do with Deputy Lawton following him.'

'Right now,' Booth said, 'I'd welcome seeing him.'

'Hopefully with another ten deputies,' Seth said.

Dalton provided a supportive grunt. Then they reverted to silence as they awaited developments.

Frank drew his men to a halt eighty yards from the ranch house but square on to the water tower. Dalton judged that Cliff could create plenty of trouble, but if they were to advance a short distance on, he could do even more damage by splaying gunfire across their backs.

Frank appeared to be aware of the possibility of an ambush as he kept the tower, barn and few other places where people could be hiding ahead of him. He beckoned for two men to dismount and explore.

These men cautiously swung down from their horses and after a brief consultation they split up. One man went to explore the barn while the second climbed up the water tower.

'Wait for Cliff to take the lead,' Dalton said, training his gun on Frank. 'Fire when he launches the assault.'

124

Seth grunted that he understood while Booth hurried across the room to join them as nobody was seeking to outflank them. They watched the man climb the ladder with his body pressed flat to the rungs and his gun aimed upwards.

He reached the top rung without Cliff showing himself and then moved to look inside. Dalton tensed, but then winced when the man swung his gun over the edge and blasted three quick shots down into the tower.

Seth and Booth looked at Dalton, but he shook his head, judging they had lost their only advantage and there was nothing they could do to help Cliff. But then the man moved up and looked down into the tower.

He looked to Frank and shook his head. Frank gestured at him to get back down to ground level.

'Why didn't he see Cliff?' Seth asked.

'Perhaps Cliff has more sense than I thought,' Dalton said. 'He must have hidden himself in there somehow.'

When the man jumped down from the bottom rung, the other man emerged from the barn shaking his head and so Frank ordered them to explore the ranch house. But with his confidence growing he along with his men edged their horses forward.

In the ranch house Dalton shot a glance at Seth and Booth, urging them to be ready. They were staying in the shadows, but they were likely to be spotted before the two men reached the house. Even so they didn't duck and instead watched the men advance.

Frank had now moved far enough forward for Cliff to be out of his eye-line and so Cliff should be able to decimate the gunslingers, if he was still alive.

'Are we still waiting for Cliff?' Booth asked.

'Sure,' Dalton said. 'The moment he starts shooting, we join him.'

Dalton repeatedly ran his gaze up to the water tower then down to the advancing men, looking for Cliff making his move or for the men showing signs of having spotted them. He was starting to wonder if Cliff might have been shot after all when he saw movement at the tower.

Cliff raised himself and peered over the top. He took in the sight of the line of riders and the two men closing on the ranch house. He looked up to the ranch house and gave a brief gesture while shrugging. The action seemed almost apologetic.

Dalton tensed as Cliff swung round to face the riders. Cliff raised his rifle up from under the rim and placed it on the edge. Then he lifted his hands to shoulder level.

'Hey, Frank!' he shouted.

As the riders swung round to look up at the tower the three men in the house glanced at each other.

'What's he doing?' Booth muttered.

'He's selling us out,' Seth said, 'that's what he's doing.'

'Then that's what Thomas tried to warn us about.'

Dalton stared up at the tower, unwilling to believe Cliff was double-crossing them. But when the riders were all facing Cliff, he edged away from the rifle and kept his hands high in what was an unmistakable gesture of surrender.

'I thought you'd stay here,' Frank said.

'I did,' Cliff shouted, 'and we can talk this out.'

'Then come down and we will.'

Cliff cast a worried glance at the ranch house. Then he lowered a shaking hand and pointed at them, but if he was planning to shout out a warning to Frank, he didn't get to speak it when with a muttered oath Seth shot at him.

The lead shattered glass before clanging off the water tower two feet below Cliff. It made the already nervous Cliff duck, but it also made the riders swing round to face them. Booth and Dalton both kept calm and as Seth continued to fire at the tower, they picked out the two men approaching on foot.

Dalton shot at the man on the left while Booth took on the right hand man. Their first volley was wild but on the second shot both men went spinning to the ground. Neither of them returned a single shot.

Before they could turn on Frank's men, they scattered. Half the riders peeled away to gallop behind the barn while the other half rode on to reach a position side-on to the ranch house. Gunfire roared from the ranch house, but none of it found a target as they hurried into hiding.

Without being asked Booth hurried across the room to the window at the back and peered out, but long moments passed without the riders appearing.

'What are they doing?' Booth muttered in irritation.

'Just wait for them to come,' Dalton said, 'and we'll fight them off.'

'And then,' Seth said, 'we'll go after Cliff.'

Booth and Dalton grunted that they agreed with this sentiment, but they silenced when Frank's men made their move. From out of their view Frank barked out his orders.

Gunfire tore out from the barn. It shattered the already broken window panes and forced Dalton and Seth to duck. When he risked looking up, it was to see that the men who had been in the barn were hurrying to the house.

Dalton loosed off a shot at them hurrying them into hiding at the side of the house. On either side of the room, the men inside tensed, expecting an assault at any moment.

Lead blasted through the back window forcing Booth to duck. Dalton looked back, but from his angle he couldn't see anyone outside, and when Booth bobbed up he didn't fire showing he couldn't see anyone either.

They got their answer as to what the plan was when

a hand emerged around the side of the window and fired inside indiscriminately. With nothing to aim at the men could do nothing but make themselves small and hope they got lucky.

The hand jerked back, but there was no respite as a second hand emerged from someone who had sneaked beneath the window. This time Booth was ready for him and he scurried along beneath the window and grabbed the arm then tugged.

He drew a man into view while he continued to fire and with a deadly accuracy Seth shot him in the chest. As more gunfire ripped out the man fell backwards, but he drew Booth up to a standing position.

Booth stood before the window, swaying.

'Get down!' Dalton shouted, but Booth remained before the window.

He walked around on the spot to face them letting Dalton see his face contorted in a grimace. His gun fell from his fingers but he didn't appear to notice it as he reached up to his stomach, where a spreading wet patch showed that the shooter had got lucky with his wild gunfire.

Booth keeled over.

Seth hurried over to take his place, but then men appeared moving into view through the window from either side and they laid down a burst of sustained gunfire that cannoned off the wall and floor. With lead flying Seth slid to a halt then turned on his heels and ran for the door.

The men followed his progress, but Seth quickly leapt through the door. Lead ripped into the wood. Then the men turned to Dalton.

In desperate self-preservation Dalton followed Seth's lead and with the door being too far away he leapt at the window. In a heap of broken glass he pitched down on to the porch, rolled, then came up on his feet and followed Seth in a dash for the only available cover of the barn.

Seth reached a point where he could see the side of the ranch and he started firing on the run. Dalton hurried on to catch up with him as gunfire tore into the ground around Seth's feet.

A cry of pain went up as Seth dispatched one man, but then a returned shot ripped into his chest spinning him round and to his knees.

Dalton hurried on to reach him and when the side of the house came into view, he saw that three men were holed up there. In an instant all three men trained their guns on him.

CHAPTER 13

Dalton threw himself to the ground as gunfire whined over his back. He slid across the ground on his side and came to rest facing towards the gunmen.

With his arms planted to the ground in a triangle to steady his aim he dispatched the nearest gunslinger. The other two men moved out from the wall to gain a better angle.

Dalton followed them and slammed a high shot into the right-hand man's chest, sending him stumbling backwards. The other man had already got Dalton in his sights, but before he could fire another gunshot rang out and the man went spinning away.

Dalton glanced to the side to see that Seth had fired. Seth cast him a glance and gave a quick shrug. Then he toppled over.

Dalton jumped to his feet and hurried to him, but when he turned him over Seth was gurgling using ragged breaths.

'Come on,' Dalton said, taking his arm. 'Let's get you to the barn.'

'I'll stay here and pick off a few more,' Seth said with a faint smile.

Dalton smiled, wondering what he could say to a man who had gone from trying to kill him to saving his life in such a short time.

'Obliged,' he said with an encouraging wink. Then he patted his shoulder and hurried to the barn.

He reached the door without anyone else coming into view then swung inside. He confirmed nobody had been lying in wait then peered out through a knothole.

Seth was lying on his side facing the house. Nobody else was in view, everyone clearly having gone behind the building. A minute passed before a man appeared in the doorway and peered outside. He saw Seth and jerked back.

Men appeared at the window and a volley of lead burst out. Dust kicked around Seth. Then he twitched and pitched over to lie on his chest, although his minimal reaction suggested he had been dead already. Then speculative gunfire splayed around the barn.

Dalton reckoned that when they came for him he could make them pay dearly, but he also reckoned he couldn't prevail in such an open space that had a second door at the back. His main hope was that he could get Frank before they overwhelmed him, but Frank tended to keep himself back and let others take the risks.

This thought made him remember that there was one other person beside Frank who he couldn't let live to enjoy the fruits of his activities. He backed away from the wall and picked out a hole in the side wall.

The water tower loomed over the barn and although he couldn't see up to the top, he remembered that Cliff had stayed down while he and Seth had fled the house. Therefore he might not know that he was here, and the tower was a better place to hole up than the barn.

After a glance outside to check that nobody was straying from the house, he headed to the back door and then around the back of the barn to reach the base of the tower. It was set on four legs with a ladder, but the ladder was rickety. If he scaled it, like the man who had climbed it earlier, he would warn Cliff he was approaching.

He went to the leg on the opposite side of the tower to the ladder. He checked that the house remained out of view then peered up.

The wooden leg was wide and irregular enough to provide handholds and when he reached the tower there were metal rivets that held the sheets together that might provide him with purchase.

Dalton holstered his gun then began climbing. He clambered up the leg without difficulty, but when he reached the metal section the exterior leaned outwards at a sharper angle than it had appeared to have at ground level. And the metal was smooth with nothing to hold on to other than the rivets.

He put a hand to a rivet and clutched his fingers around it, then drew himself up. To his relief the handhold was wide enough to support his weight and with surprising ease he worked his way upwards, but the strain on his fingers made them cramp up and so he couldn't pause for breath. He maintained the rhythm of raising his hands and placing his feet on the rivets below.

His feet dragged frequent dull clangs from the metal that were sure to warn Cliff that something was happening, but he hoped he wouldn't work out that someone was climbing the tower.

When he peered over the top he breathed a sigh of relief. Cliff was facing the house while peering from side to side at the ground looking for the source of the noise.

Dalton placed both hands on the rim and drew himself up steadily avoiding making any additional noise until his weight was resting on his arms. He glanced down to check the position of the walkway around the top of the tower. It was four feet down and beneath the walkway was the turgid dark pool of the collected water.

It would be hard to drop down silently, but Dalton gave himself every chance as he levered a leg up on to the rim. Then he swung the other leg up and rested before he lowered himself down.

He landed with bent knees, but the motion still dragged a thud from the walkway that reverberated around the tower and made ripples cascade across the water below.

Cliff swung round, his hand moving for the rifle, but he found he was facing Dalton's already drawn gun.

'Don't move another inch,' Dalton said.

Cliff lowered his hand and his head.

'I'm sorry,' he murmured.

'I gave you the benefit of the doubt once and you let me down, so I don't believe that. Speak the truth this time.'

'I was outnumbered. I. . . .' Cliff trailed off from providing his lame excuse.

Dalton sighed, unwilling to accept him but also unwilling to kill him.

'I guess all that matters is what you do now. So if I let you pick up that rifle, which direction will you aim it?'

Cliff glanced at the ranch house then at the rifle.

'I'm a dead man whatever I do,' he murmured, his voice barely audible, 'so I'll turn it on Frank.'

Cliff flashed a smile, but Dalton merely returned a harsh glare. So Cliff turned to survey the scene below.

'What's happening?' Dalton asked.

'Frank's staying in the house, but the men I can
see in the windows are looking at the barn. I don't
reckon he knows you're here.'

Cliff's voice wavered and after his previous duplic-
ity Dalton had no confidence that he had been
honest. He also noticed that beside Cliff there were
several rusted holes in the metalwork. Presumably he
had looked through these earlier while keeping
watch.

'Then we have to keep it that way.'

Dalton shuffled round the walkway bent double.
When he reached the other side he beckoned for
Cliff to back away. Then he raised himself to the
largest hole.

He had a good view of the house and barn. Several
men were approaching the tower, in direct contra-
vention of Cliff's claim. Dalton turned to confront
Cliff, but then he found that Cliff was launching
himself at him.

Dalton jerked back to the wall, avoiding Cliff's
onslaught. Cliff stumbled to his knees on the walkway
where he knelt glaring down while breathing deeply.
Dalton swung his gun round to sight him.

'Shoot me,' Cliff whispered. 'End this.'

'You're the only help I have. Don't make me.'

Cliff got to his feet. He glanced at Dalton's gun
then at the rifle lying on the rim.

Dalton nodded while providing a narrowed-eyed

warning glare. Cliff inched his hand towards the rifle while looking at the men below. He leaned forward as his gaze drifted closer to the tower while he placed a hand on the rifle.

He moved to raise it, but then a gunshot peeled out from below.

Dalton winced as blood sprayed and Cliff slid down the wall to land sitting facing him. The two men locked gazes.

'He's coming,' Cliff murmured. 'I was going to get him. I was.'

He keeled over on to his chest. Dalton didn't know whether at the last Cliff had been actually going to help him, but he patted him on the back then dragged him aside. He moved to look through the hole, but then he heard rattling on the outside of the tower.

Too late he realized what Cliff's warning had meant. A shadow moved over him and a man came springing over the side of the tower having silently clambered up the ladder. Dalton swung his gun up, but before he could fire the man rolled over the rim and dropped.

The man slammed into his chest, knocking the gun from his grip and tumbling Dalton backwards. Dalton thrust out his left hand to stop his motion, but it landed on air and, with a lurching feeling in his guts, he rolled sideways off the walkway.

He fell with the man following him then slapped

into the brackish water headfirst. He went plummeting downwards until he came to a halt several feet down.

With a wave of his arms and legs he sought buoyancy. Air was his first priority as he'd been caught unawares and he hadn't drawn in breath before hitting the water.

He came up spluttering, then looked around for his assailant. The spreading ripples where they'd both fallen was his only clue, so Dalton backed away in the water aiming to reach the walkway.

He'd covered only a few feet when hands wrapped around his legs and tugged, pulling him underwater. He kicked out, but he failed to hit his assailant and he took several flails of his limbs before he righted himself then moved back for the surface.

He emerged, shaking his head to free his eyes of water and found himself facing an onslaught. Two hands crashed down on his shoulders and shoved. Then his assailant bore down with all his weight driving him underwater.

Dalton fought to reach the surface, but the man was above him. Whichever way he turned his route was blocked. So Dalton tried the one direction that wasn't covered and kicked downwards.

His unexpected movement dragged him away from the man's grasp and he headed down towards the base of the tower. Dalton wasn't desperate for breath yet and so he swam downwards until he touched the base then looked up.

Despite the murky water he could make out the dark form of his assailant superimposed on the circle of light. He was treading water while presumably looking down for him.

Dalton reckoned he had another thirty seconds before he would have to go up for air and so he waited him out, hoping to use the element of surprise to gain an advantage.

He got an even better result when the man moved to the side. His profile became smaller as presumably he stood straight in the water, giving Dalton the impression he was reaching up to the walkway.

His dry gun was still up there and if he reached it Dalton would have no chance. Despite the urgency Dalton still acted calmly.

He swung round in the water then drew his legs up while forcing himself downwards. With both feet planted on the base, he aimed himself at the dark shape above and kicked off.

He went shooting up and came out on the surface in a fountain of water just as the man slapped a hand on the walkway. Dalton caught him around the waist and with the man's hands being thrust high he took advantage of his vulnerable state by pushing him beneath the walkway.

The man waved his arms, seeking to elbow Dalton in the face, but Dalton jerked away from the blows and slapped a hand to the back of his head. Then he drove forward and slammed his face into the side of the tower.

The man uttered a pained bleat and on the second blow he went limp. Even with him providing no resistance, Dalton took no chances. He gathered a firmer grip of his head and drove him forward for a final time with all his might.

The man's face crunched into the metal and when his body rebounded it slipped from Dalton's grip. He came to rest face down in the water with his arms spread.

Dalton edged away to stop beneath the walkway, moving cautiously in case his assailant had set his own trap. The man continued to float away. So Dalton drew himself out of the water to lie on the walkway where he wasted no time in reclaiming his gun.

After a last brief glance at the floating man, he peered outside through the hole. Several men were below gesticulating and debating. Frank wasn't among them so Dalton stayed his fire.

He watched them, noting their frequent glances at the barn then at the tower. He couldn't tell what was interesting them, but then he heard a rattle beneath him, a sound he'd heard before.

The men below would be uncertain as to whether he was up here, but he couldn't enjoy that small advantage any longer. He jumped to his feet and grabbed the end of the ladder. With a brisk tug he drew it up from the rim then shoved it forward.

The ladder was attached to one of the legs, but his shove was strong enough to break it. The top half of the ladder along with the man who had been climbing it tipped backwards then went crashing to the ground.

Dalton ducked down before any retaliatory gunfire erupted then sat back against the side. He had climbed the tower so Frank's men could too, but now that he knew what to listen for, if they tried it, he'd hear them coming.

'Hey, Frank,' he shouted, now feeling more confident of surviving than he had at any stage since he'd arrived at the ranch. 'You won't get me now.'

'You're trapped up there, Dalton,' Frank shouted back, his voice coming from the barn.

'And you're trapped down there. Deputy Lawton knows what you did to the Two Forks folk and the bridge workers. He and the railroad are on your tail and they'll be here by sundown.'

Dalton was only sure about the former element, but he figured Frank wouldn't know that.

'You won't live to see any help.' Frank laughed. 'I always burn my bridges.'

The men below laughed. Then he heard rustling below the tower.

Dalton flexed his gun hand then leapt to his feet aiming to frighten them off from whatever they were planning to do then found to his shock that they'd already done it.

A mound of wood was around the base of one of the wooden legs. Tendrils of smoke were rising up as a fire took hold.

CHAPTER 14

Dalton fired down into the base of the tower, grouping his shots in the hope of breaking through the metal and sending water pouring out, but a glance over the side showed that he hadn't managed to hole the metal.

As he didn't want to use up all his firepower on trying to put out the flames, he settled down and hoped the fire wouldn't be able to burn through the thick wooden legs. Every few minutes he raised himself to survey the horizons, but he saw no sign of anyone approaching.

Whenever he looked to the barn, Frank's men were keeping out of his sight and so he amused himself by shouting taunts, hoping to goad Frank into emerging so he could take a pot-shot at him. But Frank remained patient and out of view.

After thirty minutes two men appeared with wood and scurried into hiding beneath him. Dalton leaned over the side and splayed gunfire about. He was rewarded with a cry of pain but this didn't stop them re-stocking the fire.

The rest of the time the men stayed out of view in the barn. Dalton judged that another half-hour passed and he was starting to hope that the tower would be strong enough to withstand the fire when with a sudden crack the tower lurched.

Water sloshed up to the walkway wetting his legs and when the waves had subsided he was at an angle. He looked over the side to check the horizons, but there was still no sign of anyone coming.

He finished his perusal looking at the barn and to his delight several men had emerged in the hope that the tower was about to collapse. Dalton aimed at the nearest, but before he could loose off a shot another huge crack sounded and the tower lurched again. It swung to the side.

This time the tower didn't come to rest and it continued to topple.

Dalton gritted his teeth, hoping the tower would resettle, but with a cracking of timbers it continued to tilt letting him see the horizon, then the top of the barn. By the time he could see the ranch house it was clear the tower was going to fall and he could do nothing but hang on to the walkway and hope.

As water sluiced down on him then poured out of the top, he wrapped an arm around the side and thrust the other between two bars. The tower collapsed at a steady rate until it was at a forty-five degree angle. Then the strain on the legs became too much and it plummeted.

Dalton had a dizzying view through the top, which made him feel that it was the world tipping over and not the tower. Then, with a huge crash, the side hit the ground.

The force ripped Dalton from the walkway and threw him across the tower. He had a brief terrifying vision of the other side hurtling towards him with bone-crunching speed, but then he sliced into the moiling water. This slowed him down, but he still slammed against the side.

The surge of water pouring out of the top took him away. He went sliding along the side towards what had been the top before the tower had toppled over on to its side.

At the mercy of the deluge he went feet first towards the light until with a jarring thud he hit a solid object. With his senses swirling he had no idea what had happened, although he reckoned he was still in the tower.

Cold metal pressed against his cheek and he realized he'd fetched up on the underside of the walkway and the flow of the water was keeping him pressed there. He looped an arm around a bar and hung on. The water roared in his ears and his lungs screamed for air, but he kept his mouth tightly closed.

Within moments the water sluiced away leaving

him dangling from the walkway while he dragged in a relieved mouthful of air. He looked through the top of the tower at the water flooding out across the ground. Then he had to blink and shake himself as he failed to understand what he was seeing.

The pool of water on the ground was spreading in one direction, while a force tugged his legs in the other. Then, with a bewildering change of perspective, he saw what had happened.

The round tower had hit the ground and it was now rolling.

Slowly his legs swung round to stick out from the walkway then continued moving on. He had to shift the way he held on to the bar to avoid falling as the tower continued to revolve. Eventually the movement brought his feet up against the side and he rested for a moment before the rolling tower took his feet away.

With him no longer disorientated he looked to the top and saw the barn circling by. Frank's men were scurrying away, but one man stared in shock at the advancing structure. He jerked one way and then the other, torn between deciding which route was the safest. He chose to run away along the path of the tower, then disappeared from view.

Seeing the barn helped Dalton to work out that the tower was speeding up. There was an incline towards the house and the tower was heading down it. For how long it would roll Dalton didn't know, but the metal was screeching and flexing as if it'd collapse at any moment.

The tower completed another turn to leave Dalton's feet pressed up against the side, this time for only a brief moment before it embarked on another revolution past the barn. The water had now all sluiced out and bolts of light were springing up around him as the riveted tower came apart with a series of loud cracks.

As he continued to circle Dalton looked around for his most likely escape route. He judged that getting on the other side of the walkway then leaping out through the top was his best option.

So when his legs again swung out below the walkway he released his grip so he slipped down to the bottom of the walkway. Then he moved himself round to the other side to rest a few feet from the top.

Now he just had to throw himself clear. He watched the ground circle away from him and he judged the speed so that he could get out when the ground next came down to his side. But then with a thunderous clatter the tower screeched to a halt.

The force pressed Dalton against the walkway where he clung on, assuming the structure was collapsing, but long moments passed without the metal walls falling in. Instead, with several shudders the tower settled and silence overcame him, that quietness being eerie after the cacophony of the last few minutes.

The tower had come to rest leaving him at the topmost part. He looked down and judged the drop down to what was now the base as being too great to fall without injury, but then the opening caught his attention. He could see only a small part of the ground as the ranch house was filling most of his view.

The tower had rolled into the house and then bitten into the wall and roof. Most helpfully the middle of the tower was level with the bottom of the roof and so if he could clamber around the walkway he could jump down on to it.

Before he could begin the manoeuvre, his other major problem seized his attention. Shouting sounded. Then Frank's voice rose up and demanded that they get him.

Dalton felt his holster, but his gun had come loose, so he decided to let them come for him. He gave up on trying to reach the roof and slipped his legs up to the walkway then wrapped a knee around a bar. While clinging on, he looked down.

Presently two men came scrambling over the roof. They shuffled carefully down the shingles, clearly worried about falling through the damaged roof, while they peered into the tower.

With the bright sunlight they wouldn't find it easy to spot him in the darkened interior so Dalton stayed still. His method received the reward he'd hoped for when one man cried out then pointed down into the tower.

'There,' he said, pointing. 'The fall killed him.'

The other man looked where the first man was looking and shrugged.

'It doesn't have to be him.'

Dalton slowly moved his head round to look down into the tower and saw the body of the man who had attacked him lying on the base. Two bodies should have been in here, but presumably Cliff's had shaken loose. Dalton watched the men approach, hoping that this piece of good fortune was about to help him.

The men stopped at the area where the rim had bitten into the roof then looked for a way to climb down into the tower. This moved them into the shadows, but it also moved them to a point below Dalton.

One man pointed out the walkway and signified that he would try to climb down it. This made the second man look along the walkway, appraising how stable it was. His gaze rose until he was looking at Dalton.

They locked gazes. The man flinched with surprise when he realized that he wasn't looking at another body, but by then it was too late. Dalton swung down to dangle beneath the walkway then launched himself at the man.

Before the man could move out of the way Dalton crashed down on his shoulders sending him reeling. Both men landed on the roof, which creaked ominously. Dalton raised himself first and turned on his heels to face the second man, who stared at him in surprise while scrambling for his gun.

Dalton didn't give him a chance to draw. In two long paces he advanced on him then threw his weight behind a round-arm punch that sent the man tumbling off the roof and into the metal tower. A loud clang sounded as he landed heavily.

Dalton turned his attention to the first man. This man was getting to his feet, but he did so gingerly fearing he would break through the roof. Dalton put that concern from his mind and he pounded over to him, but just as he drawing back his fist to launch a running punch, his right foot went through the roof.

In seconds the hole expanded as more shingles gave way.

His momentum still moved him onwards and his clawing grasp took a hold of the man's jacket and yanked him forward. They both went down, but with Dalton moving away from the hole and the man moving towards it, it was his opponent who found himself in the most trouble.

The man waved his arms trying to right himself and avoid the rapidly expanding hole, but he failed and inexorably he slipped down. In desperation he drew his gun and turned it towards Dalton, but with a smile on his lips Dalton grabbed the gun and held it as the man tumbled away from him.

Dalton turned the gun in his grip then peered

down into the hole. The man was lying on his back where he'd fallen, but he wasn't moving and his head was lying at an angle that suggested a broken neck. So Dalton concentrated on getting himself out of the hole.

He holstered the gun then clamped his hands down on the roof and extricated his dangling leg from the hole. Then he lay on his side getting his breath while looking around.

Nobody was close and so he knelt and strained his neck to see what the others were doing at ground level. A scene of devastation faced him.

He'd seen that one man had failed to get out of the way of the rolling tower, but he hadn't known that others had perished when the tower had unexpectedly careened off. He counted five men lying sprawled and flattened in the mud beside the barn.

Dalton judged that most of the men who had come to the ranch had perished, perhaps including Frank Kelley, and so for the first time since he'd taken refuge in the tower he wondered if he might actually survive. With his hopes rising, he moved to the edge of the roof and looked down.

Nobody was below other than the man who had fallen off the roof, and he was lying still at the base. A dark pool of blood around his head showed that he'd fallen awkwardly.

So, slowly Dalton edged away from the holed section of roof and made his way to the side of the house, and then over the apex. All the time he surveyed the scene below, but he failed to see anyone on the ground other than the dead men by the barn.

When he'd done a complete tour of the roof and was standing beside the tower again, he looked for a way down. He still supposed that some of the men who had aligned themselves against him must be alive, but he couldn't see them. So his priority was to confirm Frank was dead then beat a hasty retreat.

He moved towards the tower, aiming to use the walkway to climb down.

'That's far enough, Dalton,' a voice said from above.

Dalton looked up. Frank Kelley was standing on the edge of the tower above him with his gun trained down on him.

CHAPTER 15

'So you survived,' Dalton said, taking a short pace backwards.

'I did.' Frank glanced around without taking his gun off him. 'But it seems we're the only ones who did.'

'Then we can end this the proper way.' Dalton took another short pace backwards to stand beneath the rim.

'We will.'

Frank raised his gun to sight Dalton's chest. He flashed a brief smile, suggesting he was about to fire and so with no time to draw and raise his gun Dalton took a long step backwards. His foot landed on the broken edge of the roof and he tumbled backwards.

A single gunshot tore out, whistling by his falling form. Then Dalton had other concerns to face.

He twisted while falling and managed to slap a hand against a dangling and broken beam. The wood stopped his fall for only a brief moment, but it was long enough for his legs to swing down and stop him plummeting headfirst.

Another shot blasted through the hole, but by then Dalton was dropping to the floor and away from Frank's line of sight. He landed with bent knees then threw himself to the side to avoid falling into a position where he could be seen from above.

He checked that the man who had fallen through the roof was dead. Then he hurried to the door.

The tower had crashed into the house to the side of the door and so when he went outside a wall of metal was to his side. He placed his back to the metal to avoid being seen from the top. Then he skirted around the side and under the bulging overhang until he reached what had once been the bottom.

He pressed his back to the metal and listened. Rustling sounded then a clang giving him the impression that Frank was climbing down the walkway. This meant he would be vulnerable and so he looked along the base.

Two sheets of metal had broken apart to his left and so he hurried to the gap. With his gun held high, he slipped through to come out within the tower. The walkway was silhouetted against the sky above the roof, but Frank wasn't on it.

Another clang sounded above. He looked up. He had got it wrong. The sound was coming from outside the tower. Frank was clambering along the top of the tower aiming to get back down to the ground.

Dalton smiled to himself and stood beside the gap planning to emerge and surprise Frank when he jumped down. He listened to him make his way towards him. Frank stopped at the edge of the rounded base as presumably he tried to judge the best way to jump down.

Scratching sounded behind him. Dalton ignored it and kept his attention on listening for Frank's progress, but then the thought came that he hadn't checked on the man who had fallen into the tower earlier.

He swung round just as two bunched fists swung down aiming to slap him on the back of the neck. He jerked away avoiding the planned blow and instead his bloodied and still groggy assailant slammed both hands into the metal wall. He screeched and wrung his hands, giving Dalton enough time to slam a bullet into him from close to.

As the man folded and collapsed at Dalton's feet, Dalton swung round to face the gap, but their altercation must have alerted Frank as silence greeted him. He risked peering out, but Frank wasn't visible.

A gunshot peeled out, making Dalton swing

round, but he couldn't see anyone within the tower. A second shot tore out and this time Dalton saw a flash as the bullet skidded off metal. He was still sure nobody else was within the tower, so he looked to the roof.

There were numerous gaps and holes created during the tower's collapse and rolling progress to the house. Frank was indiscriminately firing down through any holes he could find, hoping to catch him with a lucky shot, then quietly moving on.

Another shot blasted down. It was towards the walkway, showing that Frank didn't know where he was. Better still, Dalton glimpsed movement through a hole.

'Two can fight this type of battle,' he whispered to himself then quietly made his way to the centre of the tower below the largest hole above.

He waited for Frank to try this hole. Gunshot followed gunshot, all ripping around the tower but thankfully all landing away from him. Sometimes he caught glimpses of Frank's form, but never for long enough for him to shoot back.

'You still breathing down there?' Frank shouted. When Dalton didn't retort he continued to taunt him.

Dalton didn't mind as it was letting him keep track of his progress. He just needed patience and luck, and so he kept his gun on the one hole. That patience was rewarded when after another three wild shots, a dark form appeared above.

He fired. A screech of pain sounded then a clattering that slid down the tower. It wasn't loud enough to be Frank's body and so Dalton reckoned he'd hit Frank's hand and he'd released his gun for it to go flying away.

Confident now of having a winning advantage Dalton turned and hurried to the gap. He slipped outside then peered upwards while walking backwards, aiming to shoot the moment he saw Frank. But he'd managed only two paces when Frank leapt from the tower.

He was caught unawares as Frank slammed into him and both men went down with Frank landing on top. With Dalton winded Frank lunged for his gun hand. He slapped a hand around the wrist and squeezed, aiming to make him drop it.

Dalton tried to buck him, but Frank had squarely landed on his chest and he bore down on him, his eyes wide as he strained to hold him still. Dalton's grip of the gun loosened as Frank tightened his hand. When he looked up, he found he was holding the weapon with only two fingers and they were becoming numb.

He remembered that he had already wounded Frank and so he put the gun from his mind. With his other hand he sought out Frank's right hand. His fingers closed around a damp wrist. He tightened his grip, jabbing the fingers into the flesh.

Frank screeched in pain and jerked his hand away, but he also released his grip of Dalton's gun hand. Dalton drew it back into his grasp and with only a moment to take advantage of his weakness he slammed the gun up against Frank's side. He fired.

Frank stiffened and glared down at him.

'That was for Loren Steele,' Dalton said. He fired again. 'That was for Sheriff Blake.'

Frank rolled off him, his body limp, letting Dalton get to his feet where he continued to recite the names of everyone he knew who had died at Frank's hands.

By the time he'd finished his litany of the dead, Frank's body was a reddened slab of flesh and the sun was setting behind the hills beyond Two Forks.

The fire had ensured that there wasn't much left of Dalton's house, but then again there wasn't much left of Two Forks either.

Dalton had taken a slow ride around what had been his home for the last three years, remembering the good times and the good people. He hoped that not everyone who had taken Cliff Sinclair's money had been tracked down and killed, but even so he doubted they would return here.

The railroad bridge would be rebuilt and White Falls would boom, as would the gold mine at Durango. Maybe Two Forks would be reborn too. The area was fertile and everything that had attracted the original settlers was still here, but if a new settlement did spring up, it wouldn't be Dalton's Two Forks.

Dalton dismounted and searched through the cold embers of his former life. The heat had been intense and none of his possessions had survived. But as he was preparing to give up, a small bright object caught his eye.

He batted away charred wood to reach it and found that it was the locket he'd given to his wife Eliza a year before she'd died. Loren had helped him make that trinket from a gold nugget he'd found in the river. He'd also made a ring, but that had been buried with her.

The intense heat had distorted the metal, making it useless, like everything else here. He held it to his chest then returned to his horse. At a steady pace he rode down to the river.

On the bank he took one last look at the fast-flowing water, remembering his first sight of this place and how his heart had thudded with joy at the thought of settling here.

He hefted the locket and he was about to slip it in his pocket, but then with a flash of anger he hurled it away for it to go flying out across the river. The small golden star sank with a barely audible splash as he returned it to the place where he'd found it.

He backed his horse away. White Falls was to the

159

east. Durango was to the north. The railroad was to the south.

Dalton turned west towards the recently set sun.